CAMI KOEPP

The Weight of Fire

First edition

This book was professionally typeset on Reedsy.
Find out more at reedsy.com

Contents

1

The Clock Strikes Twice

Mara Simmons didn't believe in coincidences. So, when she stepped into the elevator on an ordinary Wednesday morning and came face-to-face with the man she'd once loved—and lost—she felt the weight of something greater than chance.

Nathaniel Nate Westwood was older now, his boyish charm honed into a quiet confidence that made him seem untouchable. His tailored gray suit fit him perfectly, and his deep-set blue eyes, once filled with laughter and mischief, were calm, almost detached.

Mara froze. Ten years had passed since that disastrous night at the spring formal—when her carefully written confession letter fell into the wrong hands, spiraling into a public humiliation that sent Nate fleeing the small town they'd grown up in. Everyone said he'd left for university in New York, but rumors swirled. She'd heard whispers of tragedy, of scandal. And now, here he was in the same corporate building where she worked as an assistant to a man who didn't know her name.

Ground floor? Nate asked, his voice smooth, polished, and painfully familiar.

Mara nodded stiffly, too stunned to speak. Her pulse thundered as she fumbled for the right response, something casual, something clever—but the elevator jolted violently, cutting off the words before they could form. The overhead lights flickered, then blinked out entirely, plunging them into darkness.

Fantastic, Nate muttered.

A small emergency bulb flickered on, casting an eerie glow over the enclosed space. Mara's breath hitched. She wanted to believe he didn't recognize her. People changed. Memories faded. And yet—

This feels oddly familiar, doesn't it? Nate said, his tone light, but his expression unreadable in the dim light.

Mara's stomach dropped. Was he teasing her? Or was this some strange coincidence? Before she could answer, a tinny voice crackled through the speaker above them.

Apologies for the inconvenience. We're experiencing a minor technical issue. Shouldn't take more than an hour.

An hour. Trapped in a box with the one man she'd spent years trying to forget. Mara's fingers clenched the strap of her bag, her knuckles white.

So, Nate said, leaning casually against the elevator wall. Do you prefer 'Mara,' or are you still going by Mary? I could never decide which one suited you better.

Her heart slammed against her ribs. He remembered.

2

A Perfect Storm

By the time the elevator was fixed, Mara's nerves were frayed, her carefully constructed walls crumbling. Nate had spent the better part of the hour talking—his voice a low hum that filled the tense silence. He didn't mention their past outright, but his every word was laced with subtext, dredging up memories she'd tried to bury.

Outside, the rain was relentless, turning the parking lot into a shallow lake. Mara darted through the downpour, her umbrella woefully inadequate. She could barely see her own car through the sheets of water, but she didn't care. She just needed to escape.

Mara! Nate's voice called out, cutting through the storm.

She turned, startled to see him standing by a sleek black sedan. His tie was gone, his shirt untucked, and he was thoroughly soaked, but he looked every bit the composed executive she wasn't.

Need a lift? he asked, his lips quirking into that infuriatingly familiar half-smile.

Her first instinct was to refuse, but the icy wind made her hesitate. Her shoes were already waterlogged, and her car was at the far end of the lot. With a sigh, she nodded, reluctantly climbing into his car.

The drive was silent at first, save for the rhythmic thud of the windshield wipers. Mara stared out the window, pretending not to notice the way Nate's eyes flicked toward her at every stoplight.

You're quieter than I remember, he said, breaking the silence.

She turned to him, her irritation bubbling over. What do you expect me to say, Nate? 'Hi, long time no see. Sorry for the years of awkwardness and unresolved feelings?'

He didn't respond immediately. When he finally spoke, his voice was softer, tinged with regret. I never meant to disappear, you know.

His words hit her like a punch to the gut. She opened her mouth to demand answers, but the car swerved sharply, and she gasped as Nate slammed on the brakes. Standing in the middle of the road was a figure in a hooded jacket, drenched but unmoving.

Stay here, Nate ordered, his voice tense.

Mara watched in stunned silence as he stepped out into the rain.

3

The Face in the Rain

The hooded figure didn't move as Nate approached. Mara leaned forward, her hands trembling as she tried to make sense of what she was seeing. Was this some kind of setup? A prank? But the air in the car was thick with something far more sinister.

Nate's voice, sharp and commanding, cut through the rain. What do you want?

The figure tilted their head, their face obscured by the hood. When they finally spoke, their voice was low and gravelly. Just a warning.

Mara barely had time to process the words before the figure pulled something from their jacket. The glint of metal caught the headlights, and her stomach twisted in fear.

Nate! she screamed, throwing open the car door.

He turned just as the figure raised the weapon—a knife, glinting cruelly in the rain. Nate lunged, his movements quick and precise, disarming the attacker with a force that startled Mara. The knife clattered to the ground, and the hooded figure cursed before disappearing into the storm.

Nate stood there for a moment, his chest heaving, the rain plastering his hair to his forehead. Mara rushed to his side, her adrenaline overpowering her sense of self-preservation.

What the hell was that? she demanded, her voice shaking.

He looked at her then, his expression unreadable. It's complicated, he said, echoing the words that had haunted her since the elevator.

Complicated? she repeated, her anger flaring. What are you not telling me, Nate?

Before he could answer, a car engine roared to life behind them, and Mara turned just in time to see the hooded figure speeding away in a battered silver sedan.

Nate grabbed her arm, pulling her toward his car. Get in. Now.

And as the storm raged on, Mara realized this was no coincidence. Fate had brought Nate back into her life—but it had also brought danger, and she was suddenly a part of it.

4

The Stranger in the Shadows

The silence in Nate's car was deafening. Rain lashed against the windows, a chaotic drumbeat that matched the pounding in Mara's chest. She stared at her reflection in the glass, her pale face distorted by the rivulets of water, but her mind was on Nate. His hands gripped the wheel with a force that made his knuckles stand out starkly. His jaw was tight, his profile hard as granite.

She couldn't ignore what she'd seen. The way he'd disarmed the stranger—it wasn't normal. It was practiced, deliberate. And now, the man who'd once been the boy she dreamed about was a stranger himself.

Nate, she said finally, her voice cutting through the storm. What just happened back there?

He didn't answer immediately. His eyes flicked to the rearview mirror, scanning the darkness behind them before accelerating.

Nate! Mara's voice rose, her frustration bubbling to the surface. Don't shut me out. I have a right to know what's going on.

His grip on the wheel tightened, and for a moment, she thought he wouldn't answer. But then he exhaled sharply and spoke, his voice low and measured.

You don't understand what you're asking, Mara.

Try me, she shot back.

He glanced at her, his blue eyes piercing in the dim light. If I tell you, you're involved. Fully involved. There's no going back.

Her stomach churned. Involved in what? Some shadowy conspiracy? A gang war? What am I supposed to think, Nate?

His lips curved into a humorless smile. I wish it were that simple.

The car skidded slightly as they rounded a bend, and Mara gripped the door handle tightly. Her pulse quickened as she realized he was driving them away from the city, the roads narrowing and darkening with every mile.

Where are we going? she demanded, her voice rising. This isn't the way to my apartment.

You're not safe there, Nate said flatly. They'll know where to find you.

Who are they? Mara's voice cracked, fear lacing her words. Nate, what have you gotten yourself into?

He didn't answer, his focus fixed on the road. Mara's mind raced, piecing together fragments of the evening: the knife, the stranger, the tension in Nate's demeanor. She felt like she was in a movie, the kind where everything goes horribly wrong for the protagonist who trusted the wrong person.

As if reading her thoughts, Nate spoke again. I need you to trust me, Mara. Just for tonight.

Trust him. The boy she'd once adored, the man who'd vanished without a trace, now reappeared with secrets and danger clinging to him like shadows. How could she trust him when he wouldn't even tell her the truth?

The car slowed, and Mara realized they were pulling into the driveway of an old house. The structure loomed in the darkness, its windows black and its edges blurred by the rain. It looked abandoned, but Nate exited the car with purpose, rounding to open her door before she could protest.

We'll be safe here, he said, ushering her inside.

Safe? Mara doubted it. The house was cold, the air damp with neglect. Nate flicked on a light, revealing a sparsely furnished living room. There was a couch, a coffee table, and not much else. No personal touches, no photographs, no signs of life.

Whose house is this? she asked warily.

Mine, he replied, locking the door behind them. For now.

For now? Mara echoed, her voice rising. Nate, you can't keep dropping cryptic hints and expect me to play along. I deserve answers!

He sighed, running a hand through his wet hair. For the first time, he looked weary, the weight of whatever he was carrying pulling him down.

Mara, he began, his voice softer now. I didn't leave all those years ago because I wanted to. Something… happened. Something I couldn't control.

Her heart twisted at the rawness in his tone. What happened?

Before he could answer, the sound of shattering glass cut through the silence. Mara screamed as a brick crashed through the window, landing on the floor amidst a spray of shards. Nate moved instantly, grabbing her and pulling her behind him.

Through the broken window, a figure stood in the rain, their face obscured by a scarf. They raised a hand in a mock salute before disappearing into the shadows.

Mara's breath came in short gasps as her knees buckled. Nate caught her, his arms steady despite the chaos around them.

This is why I couldn't tell you, he murmured, his voice grim. Because now they know you're with me.

5

The Letter That Never Came

Mara sat on the couch, her knees drawn to her chest as Nate worked to board up the broken window. His movements were efficient, his expression unreadable, but she could see the tension in his shoulders, the set of his jaw.

I should call the police, she muttered, more to herself than to him.

They won't help, Nate said without looking up. Not with this.

She frowned. What does that even mean? Nate, you're not making any sense.

He finished hammering the last nail into place and turned to face her. For a moment, he looked like he might argue, but then he sighed and sank into the armchair across from her.

Do you remember the letter? he asked, his voice quiet.

The question caught her off guard. What?

The letter you wrote, he said, his eyes meeting hers. The one you left in my locker. Do you remember what it said?

Her cheeks flushed. Of course she remembered. She'd spent hours agonizing over every word, pouring her heart onto the page. But the letter had never reached him—or so she'd thought.

You... read it? she whispered, her throat tightening.

He nodded, a faint smile tugging at his lips. Every word.

Her mind reeled. But... you never said anything. You disappeared.

It wasn't by choice, he said, his expression darkening. I wanted to—Mara, I wanted to tell you so many things. But the moment I read that letter, everything changed. My father found it before I could respond.

Your father? she echoed, confused. Why would he care about a stupid high school letter?

Nate's jaw clenched, and Mara could see the struggle in his eyes. Because he saw it as leverage. A way to control me.

Control you? She shook her head, unable to wrap her mind around what he was saying. Nate, this doesn't make sense.

Before he could answer, the distant sound of a car engine reached them, growing louder. Nate was on his feet in an instant, his hand darting to the waistband of his jeans, where Mara now noticed a gun tucked out of sight.

Stay here, he ordered, his voice low and commanding.

Mara's heart raced as she watched him disappear into the shadows of the hallway. She was left alone, the sound of the approaching car sending chills down her spine.

6

A Glimpse Through the Storm

The sound of the engine drew closer, rumbling like distant thunder, and Mara could feel the vibrations in her chest as she sat frozen on the couch. Her mind raced, replaying every cryptic thing Nate had said, every strange moment since he'd reappeared in her life. Her fingers curled tightly around the edge of a damp blanket she'd pulled over herself, her knuckles white.

Why was she here? How had she allowed herself to be dragged into whatever mess Nate was entangled in? She didn't owe him anything—certainly not her trust, not after the years of silence and the unanswered questions that had haunted her.

A loud knock at the door shattered her spiraling thoughts. Mara jumped, her heart pounding against her ribs. She stood, unsure of what to do. Nate had said to stay put, but the sound of the knock, deliberate and rhythmic, pulled her toward the door like a moth to a flame.

Mara. Nate's voice came from the hallway, sharp and commanding. Don't.

She turned to see him stepping out of the shadows, his movements quiet but purposeful. The gun was now fully visible in his hand, and the sight of it sent a chill down her spine.

Nate, she whispered, her voice trembling. Who is it?

I don't know, he replied, his eyes narrowing as he approached the door. He motioned for her to step back, and she obeyed, retreating behind the couch as he unlocked the deadbolt and opened the door just enough to see outside.

A man stood on the porch, his face partially obscured by the brim of a soaked baseball cap. He wore a leather jacket that dripped with rain, and his hands were shoved deep into his pockets.

Westwood, the man said, his voice gravelly and low. We need to talk.

Nate stiffened but didn't open the door any wider. You've got the wrong house.

The man chuckled, the sound cold and humorless. You know I don't. Let me in, or we'll have this conversation where everyone can hear.

Mara's stomach twisted. The man's presence felt dangerous, like he carried violence in his very posture. She wanted Nate to slam the door, to send him away, but instead, Nate sighed and stepped aside, letting him in.

Five minutes, Nate said, his tone clipped. And you keep your hands where I can see them.

The man stepped into the room, his eyes scanning the interior with a casual disdain that made Mara bristle. When his gaze landed on her, his eyebrows lifted slightly.

Well, well, he drawled. Didn't know you'd brought company.

She's not part of this, Nate said quickly, his voice firm. Whatever you've got to say, say it and leave.

The man smirked but didn't argue. Instead, he pulled a folded piece of paper from his jacket pocket and held it out to Nate. You're running out of time, he said. The boss isn't happy. If you don't deliver soon, she'll send someone less... polite.

Nate unfolded the paper, his jaw tightening as he read. Mara couldn't see what it said, but whatever it was, it made the color drain from Nate's face.

This wasn't the deal, Nate said, his voice low and dangerous.

The man shrugged. Deals change. You know how it works.

I can't— Nate stopped himself, his hands curling into fists. She's pushing too far.

Then maybe you should've thought of that before you got involved, the man said with a sneer. Clock's ticking, Westwood.

With that, he turned and walked out, leaving the door ajar behind him. Nate stood frozen for a moment before slamming it shut, his breathing uneven.

Nate, Mara said softly, stepping out from behind the couch. What's going on? Who was that?

He didn't answer immediately. Instead, he crumpled the paper in his hand and tossed it onto the coffee table before sinking onto the armchair, his head in his hands.

Mara, I told you this was complicated, he said finally, his voice muffled.

Complicated doesn't even begin to cover it, she snapped, her fear giving way to frustration. That man—he knows you. He knows this house. And what was on that paper? What is going on?

15

Nate looked up at her, his eyes shadowed with something that looked like guilt. I can't tell you, he said, his voice barely above a whisper.

You can't or you won't? she demanded.

His silence was answer enough.

Furious, Mara grabbed the crumpled paper from the table and smoothed it out before Nate could stop her. The words scrawled across it sent a jolt of ice down her spine:

Deliver the ledger by Friday, or we come for her next.

Her blood ran cold. Her, she whispered. Who... who does this mean?

Nate stood and reached for the paper, but she held it out of his reach, her hands shaking. Who does this mean, Nate? she repeated, her voice rising.

His jaw tightened, and when he spoke, his words were barely audible. You.

The room seemed to tilt, and Mara's knees gave out. She sank onto the couch, the paper slipping from her fingers. Her mind reeled, trying to piece together the puzzle, but the edges wouldn't align. Why was she suddenly the target of a threat? What ledger? What was Nate hiding?

I never wanted this, Nate said, his voice breaking. I didn't want you to get involved.

But I am involved, Mara said, her voice trembling with anger and fear. You brought me here. You brought this into my life. So, start talking, Nate, because I need to know what the hell is going on.

He looked at her, his expression a mixture of pain and resolve. Fine, he said

16

quietly. You want the truth? You'll get it. But I can't promise you'll like what you hear.

And with that, he began to speak.

7

The Truth Beneath the Lies

The air in the room felt heavy, thick with the weight of everything unsaid. Nate sat across from Mara, his elbows on his knees and his hands clasped tightly together as if the act of holding himself still could keep him from unraveling. Mara sat frozen, her pulse roaring in her ears, bracing herself for the truth she'd demanded.

You remember my father, Nate began, his voice low and strained. George Westwood. Everyone in town thought he was this upstanding businessman. Philanthropic, generous, all of that.

Mara nodded slowly. She remembered George Westwood, or at least the version of him that hosted charity galas and funded scholarships. She'd never met him personally, but his presence loomed large in their small town.

Nate laughed bitterly. That was the image he wanted everyone to see. Behind the curtain, though? He ran one of the most extensive illegal financial networks on the East Coast. Money laundering, blackmail, embezzlement— you name it, he was involved. And I was his heir apparent.

Mara's breath hitched. You... what?

Nate's eyes darkened. From the time I was old enough to understand numbers, my father groomed me to take over. I was supposed to learn every trick, every loophole. He made me memorize ledgers, practice forging signatures, run mock deals. I hated it, but he didn't care. He said it was 'our legacy.'

Mara shook her head, struggling to reconcile the boy she'd once known with this version of Nate. But you left. You went to New York. I thought—

I didn't leave by choice, Nate interrupted, his voice tight. The night before graduation, I found out my father had started pulling in new partners— dangerous people. He planned to use them to expand the network, and he wanted me to be the face of it. I refused.

Mara leaned forward, her heart pounding. What happened?

His jaw clenched, and he looked away, his gaze distant. We fought. I said things I shouldn't have. I threatened to go to the police if he didn't stop. He... didn't take it well.

The silence that followed was deafening. Mara's mind raced, filling in the blanks, but nothing could have prepared her for Nate's next words.

The next morning, he was dead. 'Heart attack,' they called it. Nate's voice cracked. But it wasn't. It wasn't natural. And I knew—deep down, I knew it was because of me.

Mara's breath caught in her throat. Nate...

I couldn't stay after that, he continued, his voice hollow. His partners came to me, expecting me to pick up where he left off. I panicked. I ran. I thought I could disappear, but it didn't take long for them to find me.

Mara's hands trembled as she tried to process everything he was telling her.

And now they want this... ledger? What is it?

Nate leaned back, running a hand through his hair. It's the key to everything. My father kept detailed records of every transaction, every partner, every dirty deal. If anyone got their hands on it, they'd have enough evidence to take down the entire network.

Mara frowned. But wouldn't that be a good thing? Turning it over to the authorities—

It's not that simple, Nate interrupted. The people involved... they don't just operate in the shadows. They're powerful. They have connections—political, financial, even law enforcement. If I hand over the ledger to the wrong person, it'll disappear. And they'll kill me—and anyone associated with me—just to tie up loose ends.

The words hung in the air, suffocating. Mara felt a cold dread settle over her. And now they think I'm... associated with you.

Nate's expression was pained. I didn't want that. I never wanted to involve you.

Then why bring me here? she demanded, her voice rising. Why drag me into this, Nate?

His gaze locked with hers, and for a moment, she saw something raw and vulnerable in his eyes. Because you were already involved. The moment you saw me, they noticed you. They would've gone after you whether I brought you here or not.

The truth of his words sent a chill down her spine. She thought of the hooded figure, the knife, the broken window. Even if she walked away from Nate now, there was no guarantee she'd be safe.

What do we do? she asked quietly, her voice barely above a whisper.

Nate stood, pacing the length of the room. I have a plan, he said, though the tension in his shoulders suggested otherwise. There's someone I trust—a journalist. If I can get the ledger to her, she can expose everything.

But you don't have the ledger, Mara pointed out. That's why they're after you, isn't it?

Nate stopped pacing, his back to her. I know where it is. I just… haven't had the chance to get it.

Mara frowned. Why not?

He turned to face her, his expression grim. Because getting it means walking straight into their territory. And if they catch me…

He didn't finish the sentence, but he didn't have to. Mara could fill in the blanks.

The thought of Nate risking his life—of her being caught in the crossfire—made her stomach churn. But as terrifying as the situation was, there was a part of her that couldn't abandon him. She didn't know if it was loyalty, foolishness, or something deeper, but she couldn't walk away. Not now.

I'm coming with you, she said firmly.

Nate's eyes widened. Absolutely not.

You said it yourself, she argued. I'm already involved. If I'm in danger either way, I'd rather be part of the solution.

His jaw tightened. Mara, this isn't a game. These people don't play fair. If something happens to you—

Then it's my choice, she interrupted. You don't get to decide for me, Nate. Not anymore.

For a long moment, he stared at her, a storm of emotions swirling in his eyes. Finally, he sighed, the fight draining out of him.

Fine, he said reluctantly. But if we do this, you follow my lead. No questions, no second-guessing.

Mara nodded, though her heart hammered in her chest. Deal.

As Nate began outlining the plan, Mara couldn't help but wonder if she'd just made the biggest mistake of her life. But one thing was certain: there was no turning back now.

8

Into the Lion's Den

Mara's resolve solidified as Nate laid out the plan. The tension in the room crackled like static electricity, each word carrying the weight of their precarious situation. Nate spoke in clipped, methodical sentences, his tone sharper than she'd ever heard. She realized now that this was a side of him she'd never known—a version of Nate shaped by secrets and survival.

The ledger is hidden in a storage unit downtown, Nate explained, pacing the room. I left it there years ago under a fake name, thinking no one would ever connect it to me.

Mara frowned. Why haven't they found it yet? If they've been chasing you all this time, surely they would've checked storage units.

They've been focused on me, Nate said grimly. I kept moving, stayed unpredictable. But now that they've connected us... I don't know how long it'll stay safe.

Then we have to get it tonight, Mara said, her voice steadier than she felt.

Nate stopped pacing and turned to face her. It's not that simple. The storage facility is in their territory. It's risky enough for me to go, let alone you.

I told you, Mara said, crossing her arms. I'm not sitting on the sidelines while you risk your life. I'm coming.

Nate opened his mouth to argue, but her determined expression made him pause. After a moment, he sighed and ran a hand through his hair.

Fine, he said reluctantly. But if anything feels off, you do exactly what I say. No questions, no hesitation. Understood?

Mara nodded, her pulse racing. Understood.

The city looked different at night. Shadows stretched long and ominous under the dim glow of streetlights, and the rain had slowed to a mist that clung to the air like a ghost. Nate's car moved quietly through the deserted streets, the hum of the engine the only sound in the tense silence between them.

Mara stared out the window, her thoughts a whirlwind of fear and determination. She glanced at Nate, whose jaw was set in a hard line as he navigated the labyrinth of streets. He was a study in controlled tension, but she could see the strain in his posture, the way his fingers gripped the wheel just a little too tightly.

Do you think they're watching the storage unit? Mara asked, breaking the silence.

Probably, Nate admitted. But I've got a plan for that.

Care to share?

He glanced at her, a hint of a smirk breaking through his serious demeanor. Let's just say I've learned a few tricks over the years.

Mara rolled her eyes but couldn't suppress the flicker of admiration. Despite the danger, there was something reassuring about Nate's confidence. It was enough to keep her anxiety from spiraling completely out of control.

They pulled into the parking lot of the storage facility, a nondescript building with rows of metal doors illuminated by flickering fluorescent lights. Nate parked the car in the shadows, far from the main entrance.

Stay low, he instructed as they got out. And keep quiet.

Mara followed him, her heart pounding in her chest. The air smelled damp and metallic, and every creak of the asphalt under their feet sounded deafening in the stillness.

Nate led her to a side entrance, pulling a set of lock-picking tools from his pocket. Mara watched in awe as he worked with practiced precision, the lock clicking open in seconds.

Where did you learn to do that? she whispered.

Don't ask, he muttered, pushing the door open and gesturing for her to follow.

The interior of the facility was eerily quiet, the narrow corridors lined with identical storage units. Nate moved with purpose, his eyes scanning every shadow, every corner. Mara stuck close to him, her senses on high alert.

When they reached unit 437, Nate pulled a key from his pocket—a real one this time—and unlocked the heavy metal door. He pushed it up, revealing a dimly lit space packed with cardboard boxes and old furniture.

It's in here, he said, stepping inside.

Mara followed, her gaze darting around the cluttered space. Nate moved to one of the boxes near the back and opened it, pulling out a weathered leather-bound ledger. He flipped through it quickly, his expression a mix of relief and tension.

This is it, he said, holding it up. Everything we need.

Mara barely had time to respond before a voice echoed from the corridor behind them.

Well, well. Look who finally showed up.

Her blood ran cold. She turned to see two men standing at the entrance to the unit, their faces shadowed but their postures menacing. One of them held a crowbar, and the other had a gun tucked into his waistband.

Nate stepped in front of her, shielding her with his body. We're just here to grab some old papers, he said, his tone calm but firm. No need for trouble.

The man with the gun chuckled, his teeth gleaming in the dim light. Trouble's exactly what we're here for.

Without warning, he drew the gun and pointed it at Nate. Mara's breath caught in her throat, her mind screaming at her to do something, anything. But before she could react, Nate moved.

In one fluid motion, he grabbed a rusted pipe from the pile of clutter and swung it, knocking the gun from the man's hand. Chaos erupted as the other man lunged at Nate with the crowbar, but Mara's attention was fixed on the fallen gun. Without thinking, she dove for it, her fingers closing around the cold metal.

Stop! she shouted, her voice shaking as she pointed the weapon at the two men.

They froze, their eyes narrowing as they took her in. Nate glanced at her, his expression a mixture of surprise and approval.

Let's not do anything stupid, she said, her voice steadier now. Leave. Now.

The men exchanged a look before retreating, their footsteps echoing down the corridor. Mara's hands trembled as she lowered the gun, the adrenaline crashing over her like a wave.

You okay? Nate asked, stepping toward her.

She nodded, though her legs felt like jelly. Yeah. I think so.

Nate took the gun from her gently, his touch grounding her. Let's get out of here, he said, the ledger tucked securely under his arm.

As they left the storage unit, Mara couldn't shake the feeling that this was only the beginning. The ledger was in their hands, but the danger was far from over. And as much as she hated to admit it, she was starting to wonder if she'd ever feel safe again.

9

The Cost of Secrets

Mara barely registered the drive back to Nate's safe house. Her thoughts churned as she stared out the window, the city lights smearing into long streaks of color. Her hands still trembled from holding the gun, the weight of it unfamiliar and heavy in her memory. Every time she closed her eyes, she saw the man's face, the dangerous gleam in his eyes as he threatened Nate.

When they arrived, Nate guided her inside, his hand resting lightly on her lower back. The gesture was protective, almost tender, but it did little to soothe the storm raging within her.

You did well back there, he said quietly as he locked the door behind them. That was... brave.

Brave? Mara turned to him, her voice sharp. I was terrified, Nate. I've never even held a gun before, and suddenly I'm pointing one at two men who—who probably wouldn't have thought twice about killing us.

Nate didn't respond immediately. He placed the leather ledger on the coffee table, his movements deliberate. I know. And I'm sorry you had to go through that. But you kept your head, and that might've saved both of our lives.

Mara sank onto the couch, her legs too shaky to keep her upright. This is insane, she muttered, burying her face in her hands. How did I end up here? Yesterday, my biggest problem was whether my boss noticed I was late to work. Now I'm— She gestured helplessly at the ledger. Whatever this is.

Nate sat beside her, his proximity a strange mix of comforting and unsettling. Mara, he said, his voice softer now. I never wanted this for you. But I promise you, we're going to get through it.

She looked at him, her eyes searching his face for answers. Why didn't you tell me the truth sooner? Back then, when you left... why didn't you let me in?

He hesitated, his gaze dropping to the floor. For a moment, Mara thought he wouldn't answer, but then he sighed deeply.

I didn't know how, he admitted. I was young, scared, and so caught up in my father's mess that I couldn't see a way out. I thought... I thought leaving would protect you.

Protect me? Mara's voice cracked. Do you know what it felt like, Nate? To watch you vanish without a word? To think I wasn't worth an explanation?

His expression twisted with guilt. I didn't want to hurt you.

Well, you did, she snapped, the years of bottled-up pain spilling out. You hurt me more than you'll ever know.

The room fell silent, the weight of her words hanging between them. Nate's shoulders slumped, and for the first time, he looked truly defeated.

I'm sorry, he said finally, his voice barely above a whisper. For everything.

Mara wanted to cling to her anger, to the righteous indignation that had sustained her for so long. But the raw sincerity in his voice cracked something inside her. She turned away, blinking back the sting of tears.

This doesn't make us even, she said quietly. But I guess it's a start.

The sound of Nate typing on his laptop pulled Mara from her restless thoughts later that night. She wandered into the living room, where he sat hunched over the coffee table, the ledger open beside him. His face was lit by the cold glow of the screen, his expression tense.

What are you doing? she asked, her voice groggy.

Cross-referencing, he replied without looking up. I'm trying to identify which entries in the ledger connect to active players. If I can piece together the network, we'll have a stronger case when we go to the journalist.

Mara rubbed her temples, feeling the weight of exhaustion pressing down on her. You mean if we make it that far.

We will, Nate said firmly, his fingers flying over the keyboard. I won't let anything happen to you.

She sank into the armchair opposite him, watching him work. His intensity was mesmerizing, a reminder of the boy she used to know—the one who'd always been determined to solve problems, no matter how impossible they seemed. But this wasn't high school algebra. This was life and death.

What happens after? she asked suddenly.

Nate paused, his hands hovering over the keys. After what?

After you hand over the ledger. After the network is exposed. What happens to you?

He didn't answer, and the silence was louder than any words he could've said. Mara's stomach twisted.

They won't just let you walk away, will they? she pressed.

Nate leaned back, running a hand through his hair. Probably not.

Her breath caught. Then why are you doing this?

His eyes met hers, and for a moment, she saw the vulnerability he tried so hard to hide. Because it's the right thing to do. Because if I don't, they'll keep hurting people. And because… I owe it to you.

Mara's heart clenched. She wanted to argue, to tell him that his life wasn't worth sacrificing for her or anyone else. But the determination in his gaze stopped her. He'd already made up his mind.

Later that night, Mara couldn't sleep. Her mind replayed the events of the evening, the threats, the danger, the weight of the ledger sitting on the coffee table like a bomb waiting to explode. She got up and padded into the living room, hoping the quiet would calm her racing thoughts.

She froze when she saw Nate standing by the window, his silhouette outlined by the faint glow of a streetlamp outside. His posture was tense, his shoulders rigid as he stared into the darkness.

Nate? she said softly.

He didn't turn. Someone's out there.

Her blood ran cold. What?

I saw movement, he said, his voice low and steady. They're watching us.

Mara's heart pounded as she moved to stand beside him, peering out the window. At first, she saw nothing but shadows. But then—there. A figure lingering just beyond the streetlamp's reach, their outline barely visible in the gloom.

What do we do? she whispered, her voice trembling.

Nate's jaw tightened. We stay calm. And we get ready for whatever comes next.

As the figure melted back into the darkness, Mara realized she wasn't just afraid of the danger they faced. She was afraid of what it might cost them— what it might cost her—to survive.

10

The Hunter's Patience

Mara couldn't take her eyes off the spot where the figure had stood. Her breath fogged the window as she stared into the shadows, searching for any sign of movement. The stillness of the street was unnerving, each quiet second stretching her nerves tighter.

Nate's voice broke the silence. They're testing us.

Mara turned to him, her brow furrowed. Testing us? For what?

To see how we react, Nate replied, his gaze still fixed on the window. They want to know if we're afraid, if we're ready. They're calculating their next move.

Her stomach churned. What do we do?

We make them think we're not afraid, he said simply. And we prepare.

He stepped away from the window, heading to the closet. Mara followed, her anxiety mounting as he pulled out a small duffel bag. He unzipped it to reveal a handgun, spare magazines, and a few other items she couldn't immediately identify.

Nate, she said cautiously, what exactly are we preparing for?

Whatever they throw at us, he replied, his tone clipped. He picked up the gun, checked the safety, and then handed it to her. Here.

Her eyes widened as she took a step back. No way. I'm not doing that again.

You might not have a choice, he said, his voice calm but firm. If they come after us, I need to know you can defend yourself.

Mara hesitated, her hands shaking at the memory of holding a gun earlier that evening. But the look in Nate's eyes—equal parts fear and determination—made her reach for the weapon. It felt heavier than she remembered, the weight of it pressing against her palm like a physical manifestation of her fear.

Point and shoot, Nate instructed. Don't hesitate. If it's them or you, you choose you.

She swallowed hard, nodding. Okay.

The hours stretched into an eternity as they waited. Nate paced the living room, the tension radiating from him like heat. Mara sat on the couch, the gun resting on her lap, her fingers tracing the cool metal as if familiarizing herself with it would make the prospect of using it less terrifying.

Every creak of the house, every gust of wind outside, sent her heart racing. She hated this feeling—this helpless, preyed-upon fear. She wanted to scream, to run, to do anything that might shatter the suffocating stillness. But instead, she sat and waited, her breath shallow and her nerves frayed.

Nate finally stopped pacing and dropped into the chair across from her. He leaned forward, resting his elbows on his knees and rubbing his temples. For the first time, he looked exhausted—not just physically, but in a way that spoke of years of carrying burdens too heavy for one person.

I don't know how much longer I can keep this up, he admitted quietly.

Mara blinked, surprised by his candor. You mean running?

Running, fighting, hiding… all of it, he said, his voice strained. It's like I've been holding my breath for ten years, and I'm still waiting to exhale.

She studied him, her anger and fear momentarily giving way to something softer. For all his bravado and confidence, Nate wasn't invincible. He was human, just like her—vulnerable and scared, even if he tried to hide it.

You don't have to do it alone anymore, she said softly.

He looked at her, his blue eyes searching hers. I don't want you involved, Mara.

You keep saying that, she replied, her voice firm. But the truth is, I already am. And maybe… maybe that's not such a bad thing.

Nate opened his mouth to argue, but before he could speak, the sound of glass shattering erupted from the back of the house. Both of them froze, their eyes locking in a moment of shared panic.

Then Nate moved, his instincts kicking in like a well-oiled machine. He grabbed his gun from the table and motioned for Mara to follow him. They crept down the hallway, their footsteps silent on the worn wooden floor.

The sound of footsteps came from the kitchen—slow, deliberate, and far too loud to be mistaken for the wind or an animal. Mara's pulse thundered in her ears as they reached the doorway. Nate held up a hand, signaling for her to stay back, and then peered around the corner.

A man stood in the kitchen, his back to them. He wore a dark jacket, and a knife gleamed in his hand. Nate stepped forward, his gun trained on the intruder.

Don't move, Nate commanded, his voice steady.

The man froze, his shoulders tensing. Slowly, he turned, his face obscured by the hood of his jacket. He raised his hands, the knife still gripped tightly in one of them.

You've got guts, the man said, his voice gravelly. I'll give you that.

Drop the knife, Nate ordered.

The man hesitated, his eyes flicking to Mara, who stood just behind Nate. The recognition in his gaze sent a chill down her spine.

She's cute, the man said with a smirk. Shame if something happened to her.

The words were like a spark to a powder keg. Nate's jaw tightened, and his finger hovered dangerously close to the trigger.

I said, drop the knife, Nate repeated, his voice cold as steel.

The man shrugged and tossed the knife to the ground with a clatter. Fine. But this won't end here, Westwood. You know that.

Before Nate could respond, the man lunged for the nearest window, crashing through the glass and disappearing into the night. Nate rushed to the window, gun at the ready, but the man was already gone.

Mara stood frozen, her breath coming in shallow gasps. The kitchen was a mess—glass shards littered the floor, and cold air seeped in through the broken window. But all she could focus on was the pounding of her heart and the lingering fear in her chest.

Nate turned to her, his expression a mix of frustration and concern. Are you okay?

She nodded, though her legs felt like they might give out at any moment. What... what now?

Nate's eyes darkened. Now, we stop waiting. We take the fight to them.

11

The Fight Within

Mara sat at the kitchen table, her hands clutching a steaming mug of tea Nate had insisted she drink. The heat seeped into her palms, grounding her, but the whirlwind of fear and adrenaline still raged within. She couldn't erase the smirk of the man who'd broken into the house or the way Nate had faced him with such unnerving calm.

Across the room, Nate paced with his phone pressed to his ear. His voice was low, clipped, as he spoke to someone on the other end.

Keep watching the storage facility, he said. They're closing in, and I need to know their movements.

He ended the call and turned to Mara, his expression as sharp and unyielding as a blade.

Pack a bag, he said. We're leaving.

Mara blinked. Leaving? Where? And why? You said this place was safe.

It was, Nate admitted, raking a hand through his hair. But they've found us now. Staying here is too dangerous. We need to move before they regroup.

The idea of leaving the only semi-familiar place she had left filled Mara with unease, but she nodded, knowing he was right. Her body moved on autopilot as she gathered her things, her mind spinning with questions she didn't know how to ask—or if she wanted the answers.

The night air was crisp and biting as they loaded into Nate's car. The sky above was a dense curtain of stars, indifferent to the chaos unfolding below. Mara glanced back at the house as they pulled away, its dark silhouette fading into the distance.

Where are we going? she asked after a long silence.

Somewhere they won't expect, Nate replied cryptically, his eyes focused on the road.

Mara resisted the urge to roll her eyes. And that's supposed to make me feel better?

He shot her a quick glance, a hint of a smirk tugging at his lips. You're still alive, aren't you?

Barely, she muttered, crossing her arms. Maybe next time you could try being a little less mysterious.

For a moment, Nate's expression softened, and Mara caught a glimpse of the boy she used to know—the one who used to tease her about her mismatched socks and laugh at her terrible jokes. But just as quickly, the mask of stoicism returned, and the distance between them felt insurmountable.

They drove for hours, the cityscape giving way to the sprawling emptiness of the countryside. Mara dozed fitfully, the hum of the engine lulling her into a restless sleep. When she woke, the car was pulling into the driveway of a small, secluded cabin nestled among towering trees.

This is it? she asked, her voice groggy.

For now, Nate replied, cutting the engine. It's an old family property. No one knows about it except me.

The cabin was modest but sturdy, its wooden exterior weathered by time. Inside, it smelled faintly of pine and dust, the furniture sparse but functional. Nate moved through the space with purpose, checking locks and securing windows, while Mara lingered near the doorway, her nerves still raw.

This feels... temporary, she said after a moment.

It is, Nate admitted, setting down the bag with the ledger. We're not staying here long. Just long enough to regroup.

Mara sank onto the worn couch, exhaustion weighing heavily on her. And then what? We keep running? Keep waiting for them to catch up?

Nate leaned against the wall, his arms crossed. No. We make a move before they can.

She looked up at him, her brows furrowed. What kind of move?

His jaw tightened. We draw them out. Make them think they've got the upper hand. And then we hit back.

The words sent a shiver down her spine. You're talking about... what? Fighting them? Confronting them head-on?

It's the only way, Nate said simply. They won't stop coming, Mara. Not until they get what they want—or until we make it impossible for them to keep chasing us.

Her stomach twisted. The thought of deliberately walking into danger was almost too much to bear, but she knew he was right. Running could only get them so far.

Okay, she said, her voice trembling. What do we need to do?

The next day was a flurry of preparation. Nate spent hours poring over the ledger, mapping out the web of connections it revealed. Mara helped where she could, organizing notes and cross-referencing names with news articles Nate pulled up on his laptop.

As the sun set, they sat at the small dining table, their makeshift war room scattered with papers and maps. Mara's head ached from the sheer volume of information, but a strange sense of determination had settled over her.

I think we can use this, Nate said, pointing to a name circled on the ledger. Michael Anders. He's one of their enforcers, but he's not as loyal as the others. If we can get to him, we might be able to flip him.

Flip him? Mara asked skeptically. You mean, convince him to help us?

Nate nodded. Everyone has a price. We just need to figure out his.

Mara bit her lip, her mind racing. And if he doesn't go for it?

Then we'll have to convince him another way, Nate said grimly.

The weight of what they were planning settled heavily between them. Mara had never imagined herself in a situation like this—plotting against dangerous criminals, placing her trust in a man who'd become a stranger in so many ways. And yet, she couldn't walk away. Not now.

Later that night, as Mara lay in the narrow bed in the cabin's small bedroom, she stared at the ceiling, her mind churning. She thought of her old life—the one filled with work deadlines and coffee shop visits and the occasional movie night. It felt so far away now, like a faded photograph of someone else's existence.

A soft knock on the door pulled her from her thoughts. She sat up as Nate stepped into the room, his expression unreadable.

Couldn't sleep, he said by way of explanation.

Join the club, she replied with a faint smile.

He leaned against the doorframe, his gaze thoughtful. You're stronger than you give yourself credit for, you know.

The words caught her off guard. I don't feel strong, she admitted. I feel like I'm barely holding it together.

Nate's lips quirked into a small, sad smile. That's what strength looks like sometimes.

For a moment, neither of them spoke. The silence was heavy but not uncomfortable, a fragile truce in the chaos surrounding them.

We'll get through this, Nate said finally, his voice soft but firm. I promise.

Mara wanted to believe him. But as she lay back down and watched him disappear into the shadows of the hallway, she couldn't shake the feeling that the worst was still to come.

12

The Fault in the Plan

The cabin was silent except for the faint rustle of wind through the trees and the occasional creak of the floorboards. Nate sat at the dining table, his fingers drumming a slow, methodical rhythm as he stared at the ledger. His laptop sat open beside him, its screen glowing with an incomplete map of connections between the network's players. The puzzle was maddeningly complex, a labyrinth of names, transactions, and locations, all tied to shadows that moved faster than they could track.

Mara stepped into the room, a steaming mug of coffee in her hands. She placed it in front of Nate, who gave her a brief nod of thanks. She could tell by the tightness in his shoulders and the furrow in his brow that he hadn't slept much—if at all. She hadn't either.

Find anything? she asked, sliding into the chair across from him.

Maybe, Nate replied, though his tone didn't carry much optimism. Anders has a pattern. Every two weeks, he meets with someone named Pierce at a dive bar in the city. If we can intercept him there, we might be able to corner him.

Mara frowned. Might?

Nate sighed, running a hand through his hair. It's risky. If he thinks we're a threat, he could turn violent. Or worse, he could alert the others.

Then why is he our best option? she pressed. What makes you think he'll even listen to us?

Because Anders isn't loyal, Nate said, his blue eyes locking with hers. He's in this for the money, not the cause. If we offer him something better—or scare him enough—he'll crack.

The confidence in his voice didn't completely ease Mara's worry. She hated the idea of walking into the lion's den, but she hated feeling helpless even more. They couldn't stay in the cabin forever, and the ledger was a ticking time bomb. They needed to act.

Fine, she said after a moment. When do we go?

Tomorrow night, Nate said, glancing at the clock. We need to prepare. Anders won't make this easy.

The following day was a blur of planning and practice. Nate walked Mara through every possible scenario they might face at the bar, from Anders refusing to talk to him pulling a weapon. She listened intently, her nerves fraying with every what if.

You can't hesitate, Nate said as he handed her a practice knife. If it comes down to it, you need to act quickly.

Mara held the knife awkwardly, its weight unfamiliar in her hand. I didn't sign up for this, you know.

I know, Nate said softly. But I also know you can handle it.

His faith in her was both comforting and terrifying. Mara didn't feel ready for any of this, but there was no turning back. Not now.

The bar was exactly as Nate had described—grimy, poorly lit, and packed with people who had no interest in asking questions. Mara followed Nate inside, her stomach churning with nerves. The smell of stale beer and cigarette smoke clung to the air, and the din of voices and clinking glasses made it hard to think.

There, Nate murmured, nodding toward a booth in the corner. A burly man with a scruffy beard sat slouched in the seat, a half-empty glass in front of him. His leather jacket was unzipped, revealing a gun holstered at his side.

That's Anders? Mara whispered, her heart pounding.

That's him, Nate confirmed. Stay close and let me do the talking.

They approached the booth, and Anders looked up, his expression shifting from boredom to guarded interest. He didn't move as Nate slid into the seat across from him, but his eyes flicked to Mara, sizing her up.

You lost? Anders asked, his voice gravelly.

Not at all, Nate replied smoothly. We need to talk.

Anders smirked. Do we now? And what makes you think I have anything to say to you?

Nate leaned forward, his tone dropping. Because I know who you work for. And I know you're not exactly thrilled about it.

The smirk faltered, and for a moment, Anders looked genuinely unnerved. But then he laughed, shaking his head. You've got guts, I'll give you that. But you're in over your head, pal.

Mara felt a bead of sweat trickle down her spine. She kept her hands on the edge of the table, trying to look calm even as her mind screamed at her to run.

We're offering you a way out, Nate said, his voice steady. A chance to disappear before things get worse.

Anders raised an eyebrow. Worse? You think you can scare me?

No, Nate said. But I think they can.

He slid a photo across the table—one Mara hadn't seen before. It showed a man lying facedown in an alley, blood pooling beneath him. Anders' smirk vanished completely, his face paling.

Pierce, he muttered, his hand trembling slightly as he pushed the photo away. What the hell do you know about this?

More than you want me to, Nate replied. And unless you want to end up like him, you'll listen to what I have to say.

Mara's breath caught. She hadn't realized how far Nate was willing to go to play this game, and it sent a shiver down her spine. For all his calm confidence, there was a darkness to him she hadn't seen before.

Anders stared at Nate for a long moment before finally leaning back in his seat. Fine, he said gruffly. I'm listening.

As they left the bar an hour later, Mara's legs felt like jelly. The conversation had been tense and laced with danger, but Nate had managed to convince Anders to cooperate—at least for now. They had a name, a meeting point, and the faintest glimmer of hope.

But as they stepped into the cool night air, Mara couldn't shake the feeling that they were being watched. She glanced over her shoulder, her eyes scanning the shadows for any sign of movement.

Nate, she whispered. Something's not right.

Before he could respond, a car screeched to a halt at the curb, its headlights blinding them. The doors flew open, and three men jumped out, their faces obscured by masks.

Run! Nate shouted, grabbing her arm.

They darted down the alley, the sound of footsteps and shouted commands echoing behind them. Mara's chest burned as she struggled to keep up, her heart pounding with the realization that the danger they'd been preparing for was no longer a distant threat—it was here, and it was relentless.

13

Into the Shadows

The alley stretched ahead of them like a labyrinth carved from darkness. Nate's hand was firm on Mara's arm as they ran, the sound of their pursuers' heavy footsteps and barked commands reverberating off the walls behind them. The air was thick with the acrid smell of oil and trash, but Mara barely noticed, her senses consumed by the primal need to survive.

This way! Nate hissed, tugging her sharply to the right. They plunged into a narrower passageway, the walls closing in around them like the jaws of a trap.

Mara's lungs burned as she fought to keep up, her legs straining with every step. Her mind raced, torn between the instinct to panic and the need to stay focused. She'd never been in a situation like this before—never imagined she could be hunted like an animal through the city streets.

Where are we going? she gasped.

Just keep moving! Nate's voice was a sharp command, brooking no argument.

Behind them, the sound of their pursuers grew louder. Mara risked a glance over her shoulder and saw shadows stretching toward them, the figures growing larger with every passing second. Her heart pounded as she realized how close they were.

Nate! she cried.

He didn't hesitate. With a single, fluid motion, he spun around, pulling her behind him. His gun was in his hand before she could process what was happening.

The first shot cracked through the air like thunder, the flash illuminating the alley for a split second. One of the masked men staggered back, clutching his shoulder, and fell to the ground. The others slowed but didn't retreat, their determination chilling in its intensity.

Go! Nate barked, firing another shot.

Mara's legs moved before her brain could catch up, carrying her deeper into the maze of alleys. She heard Nate's footsteps pounding behind her, followed by the shouts of their attackers and the sharp crack of gunfire. Her chest heaved as she turned corner after corner, praying she wasn't running straight into another trap.

Finally, she saw a metal door set into the wall ahead of them, its surface rusted and weathered. Nate reached it first, slamming his shoulder into the door to force it open.

Inside! he ordered, grabbing her wrist and pulling her through.

The door groaned shut behind them, and Nate slid the bolt into place just as fists began pounding on the other side. The noise was deafening, a chaotic symphony of rage and desperation. Mara stumbled back, her chest heaving as she struggled to catch her breath.

That won't hold them for long, she managed, her voice trembling.

It doesn't have to, Nate replied, his eyes scanning the dimly lit space. They were in what looked like an abandoned warehouse, the cavernous room filled with rusting machinery and stacks of wooden crates.

Over here, he said, leading her toward the back of the room.

Mara followed, her pulse racing as she heard the unmistakable sound of the door starting to give way. The wood splintered under the relentless assault, and she knew it was only a matter of seconds before their pursuers broke through.

Nate stopped near a large stack of crates and crouched down, pulling a metal grate free from the floor. A narrow shaft descended into darkness, the faint smell of damp earth wafting up to meet them.

In, Nate said, gesturing toward the opening.

Mara hesitated, her stomach churning at the thought of descending into the unknown. But the sound of the door finally bursting open erased any doubts she had. She dropped into the shaft, her hands and knees scraping against the rough metal rungs of a ladder as she climbed down.

Nate followed, pulling the grate back into place above them just as the sound of boots filled the warehouse. The darkness closed in around them, broken only by the faint glow of Nate's flashlight as he switched it on.

The tunnel was narrow and suffocating, the air thick and stale. Mara's breaths came in short gasps as she followed Nate through the winding passage, her mind replaying the events of the last few minutes in a frantic loop.

Where does this lead? she asked, her voice barely above a whisper.

Out, Nate replied, his tone clipped. Keep moving.

After what felt like an eternity, they emerged into an overgrown lot on the outskirts of the city. The cool night air was a welcome relief after the suffocating confines of the tunnel, but Mara's relief was short-lived. They were still in danger, and the weight of that realization pressed heavily on her.

How did they find us? she asked as Nate led her toward a parked car hidden beneath a tarp.

They must have followed us from the bar, Nate said grimly. Or Anders tipped them off.

Mara's stomach churned. But he agreed to help us. He said—

He said what he needed to say to survive, Nate interrupted, pulling the tarp off the car. We can't trust anyone right now.

The words stung, but Mara knew he was right. They were alone in this fight, and the enemy was relentless.

As they got into the car and sped away from the lot, Mara couldn't help but glance at Nate. His jaw was set, his eyes cold and focused. She wanted to say something—to ask how he managed to stay so composed, to tell him she was terrified—but the words wouldn't come.

Instead, she stared out the window, the city lights blurring into streaks as they disappeared into the night. The weight of the ledger in her bag felt heavier than ever, a constant reminder of the danger that followed them like a shadow.

14

The Price of Loyalty

The car raced down the empty highway, its tires humming against the asphalt. Mara sat rigid in her seat, her eyes fixed on the side mirror as if the enemy's headlights might appear at any moment. The weight of exhaustion pulled at her, but fear kept her alert.

How do you know we're safe here? she asked, her voice thin in the silence.

Nate's hands tightened on the wheel, his knuckles white against the leather. We're not. But this stretch of road gives us options. If they're following us, I'll see them before they get close.

The cold pragmatism in his voice made her shiver. Mara couldn't help but marvel—and worry—at how methodical Nate had become. He didn't flinch, didn't hesitate. His instincts were sharp, almost unnervingly so, and she wondered what it had cost him to become this way.

I don't understand why Anders would betray us, she said, more to herself than to him. He looked scared enough back at the bar.

Scared men are dangerous, Nate replied. They do what they think will keep them alive, even if it means turning on someone who could help them.

Then why did you trust him?

I didn't, Nate admitted, his gaze fixed on the road. But we needed a lead, and he was the best option we had.

Mara shook her head, frustration bubbling beneath her fear. So what now? We've got the ledger, but it feels like we're no closer to ending this.

We will be, Nate said, his voice firm. I have a contact—someone I've worked with before. If anyone can help us take this thing apart, it's him.

Who is he?

Nate hesitated, his fingers drumming a tense rhythm on the steering wheel. James Grayson. Ex-military. He's… resourceful.

And you trust him?

As much as I trust anyone, Nate said, his jaw tightening. Which isn't much.

Mara sighed, leaning her head against the window. The glass was cool against her skin, a stark contrast to the heat radiating from her fear. She wanted to believe Nate had a plan, that they weren't just stumbling from one desperate situation to the next. But the more she thought about it, the more impossible it all seemed.

An hour later, they pulled into a desolate truck stop on the edge of a wooded area. The lights from the gas station cast long shadows over the lot, and the hum of an ancient neon sign buzzed faintly in the distance. Nate parked near the back, far from the pumps and the diner where a handful of truckers lingered over late-night coffee.

Wait here, he said, reaching for his phone. I need to make a call.

Wait—why can't you call him from the car? Mara asked, her voice rising slightly.

Because I don't want anyone tracing it, Nate replied, opening the door. This place has a payphone. It's safer.

Before she could argue, he was gone, his silhouette disappearing into the shadows. Mara slumped back in her seat, her frustration mounting. She hated the helplessness she felt, the constant waiting and running with no end in sight. She hated that she relied on Nate for everything when she didn't fully understand the scope of what they were up against.

Her thoughts were interrupted by a sharp knock on the passenger window. She jumped, her heart leaping into her throat as she turned to see a man standing there, his face obscured by the darkness.

Hey, miss, the man called, his voice muffled through the glass. You okay in there?

Mara's hand instinctively went to the door lock. She didn't answer, her pulse hammering in her ears.

Don't worry, the man said, holding up his hands in a placating gesture. I'm not here to hurt you. Just thought you looked a little lost.

Something about his tone set her on edge. She glanced toward the diner, hoping to see Nate returning, but the lot was still empty. She reached for the gun Nate had insisted she keep within reach, her fingers closing around the cool metal.

I'm fine, she said finally, her voice steadier than she felt. Thanks.

The man tilted his head, his hands still raised. Alright. Just thought I'd check.

You never know who you might run into out here.

As he stepped back, the dim light from the gas station illuminated his face—and the unmistakable smirk of the man who'd broken into the cabin the night before.

Mara's blood turned to ice. She raised the gun, pointing it at the window. Get back! she shouted, her voice shaking.

The man's smirk widened, but he obeyed, raising his hands higher. Easy there, sweetheart. No need to get trigger-happy.

The sound of hurried footsteps behind the car made her whip her head around. Nate appeared out of the shadows, his gun already drawn. He moved with the precision of someone who'd done this before, his aim steady as he approached the man.

Move, Nate ordered, his voice cold and commanding.

The man hesitated, his smirk faltering. You wouldn't shoot me here, he said, though his tone lacked confidence. Too many witnesses.

Try me, Nate growled, his finger hovering over the trigger.

For a tense moment, no one moved. Then the man stepped back, his hands still raised. This isn't over, Westwood, he said, his smirk returning. You can run all you want, but you can't hide forever.

Nate didn't respond, his gun trained on the man as he backed away. When the man was out of sight, Nate turned to Mara, his expression hard. Are you okay?

She nodded, though her hands still trembled as she lowered the gun. That was him, wasn't it? The one from the cabin.

Yeah, Nate said grimly, his eyes scanning the lot. He's not working alone. We need to go—now.

As they sped away from the truck stop, Mara couldn't shake the image of the man's smirk or the warning in his voice. The danger felt closer than ever, an unrelenting shadow that refused to let them go.

Nate, she said quietly, breaking the tense silence. What if they're right? What if we can't outrun them?

Nate's jaw tightened, but he didn't look at her. Then we stop running, he said. And we make them wish they'd never come after us.

Mara wanted to believe him. But as the car raced into the night, she couldn't help but feel like the clock was ticking—and they were running out of time.

15

The Alliance of Desperation

The road seemed endless as the car cut through the darkness, the hum of the engine the only sound. Mara sat silently, her thoughts spinning with questions she couldn't bring herself to ask. She clutched the gun Nate had handed back to her, the cold metal a weight she couldn't ignore.

You're quiet, Nate said, his eyes still fixed on the road.

What's there to say? she replied, her voice laced with frustration. We're being hunted like animals, we can't trust anyone, and now I'm supposed to believe you've got some mysterious contact who can help us.

Nate's grip on the wheel tightened. I told you, James Grayson is solid. He's been off the grid for years, and if anyone knows how to dismantle something like this, it's him.

And why exactly would he help us? Mara pressed. What's in it for him?

Let's just say we have a history, Nate said, his tone shutting down the conversation.

Mara sighed, leaning her head against the window. She hated the secrecy, the constant drip of half-truths. But as much as she wanted to push, she knew now wasn't the time.

Hours later, they pulled into a secluded stretch of forest. The road was little more than a dirt path, the car bouncing over roots and uneven ground. Mara's unease grew with every passing minute, the thick canopy of trees swallowing the faint light of dawn.

Where are we? she asked, breaking the tense silence.

Grayson's place, Nate replied, cutting the engine. Stay close.

Mara followed him as they climbed out of the car, her breath visible in the crisp morning air. The forest was eerily quiet, the kind of silence that made her feel like they were being watched. She clutched the gun tightly, her fingers numb from the cold.

Nate led her to a clearing where a small cabin stood, its wooden exterior weathered but sturdy. Smoke curled from the chimney, and the faint scent of pine hung in the air.

He's here, Nate muttered, striding toward the door.

Before he could knock, the door swung open, revealing a man who looked like he'd stepped out of a survivalist magazine. His beard was thick and unkempt, his clothes practical and rugged, and his eyes sharp and calculating.

Nate Westwood, the man said, his voice gravelly. Didn't think I'd ever see you again.

Grayson, Nate replied, his tone even. We need your help.

Grayson's gaze flicked to Mara, his brow furrowing. And who's this?

Mara, Nate said, his tone making it clear that further explanation would have to wait. Can we come in?

Grayson hesitated for a moment before stepping aside. Make it quick. I don't like company.

The cabin was sparse but well-maintained, the interior dominated by a large table covered in maps, weapons, and equipment. Grayson motioned for them to sit, then leaned against the wall, crossing his arms.

So, he said, his eyes narrowing. What kind of trouble are you in this time?

Nate pulled the ledger from his bag and placed it on the table. Grayson raised an eyebrow but didn't move to touch it.

This, Nate said, his voice low. It's everything we need to take down the network. Names, transactions, locations—it's all here.

Grayson stared at the ledger for a long moment before finally speaking. And you brought it to me because…?

Because I need your help, Nate replied. This isn't just about taking down the network. It's about surviving long enough to do it.

Grayson's gaze shifted to Mara. And you're involved in this why?

Mara bristled at his tone but held her ground. Because they think I am, she said. And because Nate dragged me into it.

Grayson smirked, though there was no humor in it. Well, that's Nate for you. Always good at making friends.

Grayson, Nate said, his patience wearing thin. Are you in or not?

Grayson sighed, running a hand through his beard. I'm in, he said finally. But you'd better have a damn good plan, because once we start this, there's no going back.

For the next several hours, the three of them worked tirelessly, poring over the ledger and strategizing their next move. Grayson's expertise was apparent—he spotted connections and vulnerabilities Nate and Mara hadn't even considered.

Their weakest point is here, Grayson said, tapping a name on the ledger. Marcus Hargrove. Mid-level player, handles logistics. If we can disrupt his operation, it'll send ripples through the entire network.

And how do we get to him? Mara asked.

Grayson grinned, a glint of mischief in his eyes. Leave that to me.

Nate leaned back, his expression thoughtful. If we hit Hargrove, they'll retaliate. We need to be ready.

That's where you come in, Grayson said, clapping him on the shoulder. You've always been good at playing defense.

Mara watched their exchange, a strange mix of admiration and apprehension bubbling within her. Grayson was clearly capable, but his cavalier attitude unnerved her. This wasn't a game, and the stakes were too high to leave anything to chance.

That night, as they prepared for the mission, Mara found herself alone with Nate by the fire. The crackling flames cast flickering shadows across his face, softening the hard edges she'd grown accustomed to.

Do you trust him? she asked quietly.

Grayson? Nate shrugged. I trust him to look out for himself. And right now, that means helping us.

That's not exactly comforting, Mara muttered.

It's the truth, Nate said, his gaze meeting hers. This isn't about comfort, Mara. It's about survival.

She sighed, wrapping her arms around herself. I'm scared, Nate.

I know, he said softly. So am I.

The admission caught her off guard, and for a moment, the walls between them seemed to crumble. She wanted to reach out, to tell him that they could face this together. But the weight of everything left unsaid held her back.

Instead, she looked into the fire, the flickering flames reflecting the chaos in her heart.

Tomorrow, they would face Hargrove. And whether they succeeded or failed, nothing would ever be the same.

16

The First Strike

The morning dawned cold and gray, the forest bathed in a pale light that felt more foreboding than comforting. Mara stood outside the cabin, her breath curling in soft white clouds as she watched Nate and Grayson load the last of their supplies into an old, beat-up truck. The plan was simple enough on paper—disrupt Marcus Hargrove's operation and force the network to scramble. But the simplicity of the plan belied the danger. One wrong move could get them all killed.

You ready for this? Nate asked, his voice breaking through her thoughts.

Mara turned to him, her fingers brushing against the gun holstered at her hip. I don't think I'll ever be ready.

Good, Nate said, his expression serious. Fear keeps you sharp. Just don't let it paralyze you.

Grayson approached, his rugged face creased with a grin that didn't reach his eyes. Relax, sweetheart. It's a simple in-and-out job. We're just here to make a mess and leave. Nothing to it.

Mara shot him a look. That's easy for you to say. You've done this before.

And that's why you're lucky to have me, Grayson replied, clapping Nate on the shoulder. Now let's get moving. Time's wasting.

The drive to the target location was tense. Grayson had pinpointed a warehouse on the outskirts of the city, a key hub for Hargrove's logistics operation. Disrupting it would be more than an inconvenience—it would be a statement. Mara sat in the back seat of the truck, her stomach twisting into knots as they approached the warehouse district. The closer they got, the more her fear turned into adrenaline, sharpening her senses and quickening her pulse.

Alright, Grayson said as he parked the truck behind an abandoned building. He spread a crude map across the dashboard, pointing to a cluster of red Xs. We hit them here, here, and here. Explosives on the generators, sabotage on the supply vehicles, and a good old-fashioned hard drive wipe in their office. The goal is chaos. No fatalities unless it's unavoidable.

Got it, Nate said, his voice calm but resolute.

Mara swallowed hard. And what do you want me to do?

Grayson's grin returned, though it was less mocking this time. You're with me. We'll handle the office. Nate's on explosives.

Mara glanced at Nate, her eyes widening. Explosives?

I'll be fine, Nate assured her, though his jaw tightened as he said it. Just focus on your part. Grayson knows what he's doing.

That's debatable, Mara muttered, earning a chuckle from Grayson.

The warehouse loomed ahead, its corrugated metal walls streaked with rust. A chain-link fence surrounded the property, topped with barbed wire that glinted in the dim morning light. Grayson led them to a gap in the fence, the hole just large enough for them to slip through. Mara's heart pounded as they crept across the gravel lot, the sound of her own breathing deafening in the silence.

Nate broke off first, heading toward the generators near the side of the building. He moved with a precision that reminded Mara of a panther—silent, controlled, deadly. She and Grayson continued toward the office, ducking behind a stack of crates as a guard strolled past, his flashlight cutting through the shadows.

You're doing great, Grayson whispered, his tone surprisingly genuine. Just a little farther.

Mara nodded, though her grip on her gun tightened. She hated how exposed they felt, every step a gamble against being spotted. When they reached the office door, Grayson pulled out a set of tools and began picking the lock.

Keep watch, he murmured.

Mara turned, her eyes scanning the lot as the faint click of the lock-picking filled the air. She could see Nate in the distance, crouched near the generator as he set the explosives. Her stomach clenched at the sight of him—so vulnerable, so alone.

The door swung open, and Grayson gestured for her to follow. The office was small and cluttered, its walls lined with shelves of files and computer monitors glowing faintly in the dim light.

Find anything that looks important, Grayson said, moving to the computer. I'll handle the drives.

Mara began rifling through the shelves, her hands shaking slightly as she sorted through folders and papers. Most of it was mundane—shipping manifests, inventory lists—but then she found something that made her blood run cold. A folder labeled Westwood.

Nate's name is here, she whispered, holding up the folder.

Grayson glanced at her, his brow furrowing. Bring it. We'll figure it out later.

Suddenly, the sound of footsteps echoed outside the door. Mara froze, her heart leaping into her throat as the doorknob rattled. Grayson was on his feet in an instant, his gun drawn as the door creaked open.

The guard barely had time to react before Grayson slammed the butt of his gun into the man's temple, sending him crumpling to the floor.

Let's go, Grayson said, his voice urgent. We're out of time.

The chaos erupted almost as soon as they exited the office. An explosion rocked the far side of the warehouse, the ground trembling beneath their feet. Mara turned to see flames licking at the generators, black smoke billowing into the sky.

Perfect timing, Grayson muttered, grabbing her arm. Come on!

They ran toward the fence, weaving through the maze of crates and vehicles as alarms blared and guards shouted. Mara could see Nate ahead of them, sprinting toward the gap in the fence with a determined look on his face.

But then, out of the corner of her eye, she saw movement—a group of guards emerging from the shadows, their guns trained on Nate.

No! Mara screamed, raising her gun.

She fired without thinking, the recoil jolting her arm as the shot rang out. One of the guards stumbled, clutching his leg, but the others kept advancing. Grayson fired as well, his shots precise and deadly, dropping two more guards before they could react.

Nate reached the fence, his eyes wide with relief as Mara and Grayson caught up to him. Together, they slipped through the gap and bolted toward the truck, the sound of pursuit fading behind them.

Back on the road, the adrenaline began to wear off, leaving Mara trembling with exhaustion and fear. Nate sat beside her in the truck, his expression grim as he stared out the window.

You saved my life, he said quietly.

Mara looked at him, her chest tightening. You've saved mine enough times. I figured it was only fair.

Nate's lips quirked into a faint smile, but it didn't reach his eyes. This was just the beginning, he said. They'll come for us harder now.

Mara nodded, her resolve hardening. Then we'll be ready.

Grayson chuckled from the driver's seat. You two are something else. Just make sure you don't get yourselves killed before the real fight starts.

As the truck sped into the night, Mara clutched the folder with Nate's name on it, her mind racing with questions. The operation had been a success, but the danger was far from over—and the secrets they were uncovering were more dangerous than she'd imagined.

17

The Secrets We Carry

The truck's cabin was thick with silence as Grayson drove, his eyes fixed on the road. The chaos of the warehouse was behind them, but its echoes lingered in Mara's chest—a pounding reminder of how close they'd come to disaster. The folder in her lap felt heavier with each passing mile, the name Westwood scrawled across its front in bold black ink.

Nate sat beside her, his jaw tight and his arms crossed. The faint scent of smoke clung to his jacket, a reminder of the explosions they'd left behind.

We should talk about this, Mara said, breaking the silence.

Nate turned to her, his expression unreadable. About what?

She held up the folder. This. Your name's in here, Nate. They're keeping tabs on you.

Grayson let out a low whistle from the driver's seat. Well, that's no surprise. You've been a thorn in their side for years. I'm amazed they didn't plaster your face on wanted posters.

It's not funny, Mara snapped. This could be important.

Nate reached for the folder, but Mara pulled it back. Not until you explain why your name is in it.

His brows furrowed, a flicker of irritation crossing his face. Mara, now's not the time for twenty questions.

Now's the perfect time, she shot back. We're stuck in this truck for hours, and I think I deserve some answers.

Grayson smirked, though his eyes remained on the road. She's got you there, Westwood.

Nate sighed, leaning back in his seat. Fine. Open it.

Mara hesitated, her fingers trembling slightly as she flipped open the folder. The first page was a photograph of Nate—an old one, taken long before the wear of the last decade had etched itself into his features. Beneath the photo was a list of notes in crisp, precise handwriting:

- **Westwood, Nathaniel.**
- **Son of George Westwood.**
- **Former heir to the network.**
- **Current status: rogue.**
- **Priority: high.**

What does 'heir to the network' mean? Mara asked, her eyes narrowing.

Nate's jaw tightened. It's exactly what it sounds like. My father built the network, and for a long time, everyone expected me to take his place.

Grayson let out a low chuckle. Bet that didn't go over well.

It didn't, Nate said flatly. When I refused, I became a liability. And when my father died... they decided I was a loose end they couldn't afford.

Mara's stomach churned as she read further. The file detailed Nate's movements over the past several years, piecing together a fragmented picture of his life in hiding. It also listed known associates—many of whom had been crossed out with the chilling notation: Neutralized.

She looked up at him, her voice trembling. This is why you've been running?

Nate nodded, his eyes shadowed. They don't just want the ledger, Mara. They want me gone.

Grayson whistled again, his tone low. Looks like you're not just a thorn in their side, buddy. You're the whole damn forest.

This isn't a joke, Nate snapped, his frustration spilling over. Every name in that folder—every person they've tracked because of me—they're all dead. That's what we're up against.

The weight of his words settled heavily over them. Mara stared at the file, her fingers tightening around the edges of the paper.

Then we can't let this keep happening, she said softly. We have to stop them.

Nate glanced at her, his expression softening. We will. But it's not going to be easy.

It never is, Grayson muttered. But you're lucky you've got me. I'm the kind of guy who thrives on impossible odds.

Mara rolled her eyes, but the corner of her mouth twitched in a reluctant smile. Grayson's humor, misplaced as it often was, felt like a lifeline in the suffocating tension.

They arrived at their new hideout—a dilapidated farmhouse on the edge of an overgrown field—just as the sun began to set. Grayson parked the truck behind the barn, killing the engine and stretching as he climbed out.

Home sweet home, he said, gesturing toward the house. Not much, but it's off the radar.

Mara followed Nate inside, the creaking floorboards and peeling wallpaper adding to the sense of abandonment. It wasn't comforting, but it was better than the suffocating fear of the warehouse.

What's the plan now? she asked, dropping her bag onto the floor.

Nate rubbed the back of his neck, his expression pensive. We focus on Hargrove. Grayson's intel says he'll be scrambling to recover after tonight. That gives us a window to hit his primary operation.

And where is that? Mara asked.

Grayson leaned against the doorway, arms crossed. A shipping yard on the river. It's where he moves the bulk of the network's contraband. Take that out, and he's crippled.

How do we get in? Mara pressed.

Nate and Grayson exchanged a glance before Nate answered. We'll need to infiltrate. Posing as contractors or new recruits might work, but it's risky. They'll be on high alert after what we just pulled.

And if we're caught? she asked, her voice quiet.

Then we make sure we're not, Nate said firmly. We can't afford to fail.

Mara swallowed hard, the weight of the mission pressing down on her. The ledger, the file, the network—it all felt overwhelming, a tangled web of danger and deception. But as she looked at Nate, his determination unwavering, she felt a flicker of hope.

Alright, she said. Let's do this.

Later that night, as the others slept, Mara sat by the window, the file still clutched in her hands. The photograph of Nate stared back at her, his younger self exuding a confidence she'd rarely seen in the man he'd become. She wondered what it had cost him to survive, how much of himself he'd sacrificed to stay one step ahead.

She glanced toward the corner where Nate lay on a makeshift bed, his breathing deep and steady. For all his strength and resolve, he looked vulnerable in sleep, the weight of his burdens momentarily lifted.

Mara folded the file and placed it back in her bag, her resolve hardening. She didn't know how this would end, but she knew one thing for certain—she wouldn't let him face it alone.

18

The Edge of Deception

The farmhouse felt like a hollow shell as dawn broke over the horizon, its silence amplifying the weight of the mission ahead. Nate and Grayson were in the kitchen, leaning over a crude map of the shipping yard, their voices low and clipped. Mara hovered by the doorway, her stomach churning with unease as she watched them strategize.

It's heavily patrolled, Grayson said, tracing a route with his finger. The main gate's out. Too many eyes. We'll need to get in through the water.

The river? Nate frowned. They'll have patrol boats.

Not where we're going, Grayson replied with a smug grin. There's a drainage tunnel that leads straight into the yard. It's tight, but it'll get us inside without anyone noticing.

Mara stepped forward, her voice hesitant. And once we're inside? What's the plan?

We split up, Nate said, glancing at her. Grayson and I will handle the sabotage—take out the shipment, disable their vehicles, and disrupt their comms. You'll stay back and keep watch.

Keep watch? Mara's eyes narrowed. That's it? I can do more than that, Nate.

This isn't up for debate, Nate said, his tone firm. The fewer moving parts, the better. You're safer on the perimeter.

I'm not interested in being safe, she shot back. I'm interested in helping.

Grayson chuckled, though it lacked humor. You two sound like an old married couple. How about we focus on not getting killed?

Nate sighed, rubbing the back of his neck. Fine. You can back me up. But you stay close, and if I say run, you run. Got it?

Mara nodded, her heart pounding. Got it.

By the time they reached the drainage tunnel, the sun had dipped below the horizon, plunging the world into darkness. The air was thick with the smell of oil and saltwater, the faint sounds of the shipping yard drifting toward them like ghosts of the chaos to come.

Grayson led the way, a flashlight in one hand and a gun in the other. The tunnel was damp and claustrophobic, water pooling around their boots as they trudged through the narrow passage. Mara's breaths came shallow and fast, her fingers gripping her weapon tightly as she tried to ignore the oppressive weight of the walls around them.

Almost there, Grayson muttered, his voice echoing off the concrete.

They emerged into a shadowed alcove at the edge of the yard, the roar of machinery and the shouts of workers filling the air. Massive shipping containers loomed like metal giants, their surfaces rusted and worn. Floodlights illuminated the yard in harsh beams, creating pools of light that felt almost surgical in their precision.

Nate crouched low, motioning for Mara to follow. Stay in the shadows. Don't move unless I tell you.

She nodded, her heart pounding as they crept toward the first set of containers. Grayson veered off to the left, his movements quiet and deliberate as he disappeared into the maze of metal.

What's he doing? Mara whispered.

Setting charges, Nate replied. We hit their supply lines first. No supplies, no operation.

The minutes stretched into an eternity as they moved from container to container, planting explosives and disabling equipment. Mara's senses were on high alert, every shadow and sound a potential threat. She could feel the tension radiating off Nate, his focus unwavering as he worked.

They were halfway through the yard when a voice shattered the quiet.

Hey! Who's there?

Mara froze, her breath catching in her throat. A guard stood a few feet away, his flashlight cutting through the darkness. His hand hovered over the radio clipped to his shoulder.

Nate didn't hesitate. He stepped forward, his gun raised. Don't move.

The guard's eyes widened, his hand darting toward the radio. Nate fired, the shot ringing out like a thunderclap. The guard crumpled to the ground, the radio skittering across the concrete.

Mara stared at the body, her stomach churning. Did you have to—?

He would've alerted the whole yard, Nate said sharply. We don't have time for hesitation, Mara.

She nodded, swallowing hard as she forced herself to look away. They pressed on, the weight of the mission heavier than ever.

When they regrouped with Grayson, the explosives were in place, and the shipping yard was eerily quiet. The workers had dispersed, their shifts ending just as the operation began. Grayson grinned as he held up a detonator.

All set, he said. Let's light this place up.

Not yet, Nate said, his gaze sweeping the yard. We need to make sure Hargrove's shipment is here first.

Grayson's grin faded. You think they moved it?

It's possible, Nate replied. Check the main office. If it's not here, we need to know where it went.

Grayson nodded, disappearing into the shadows once again. Mara and Nate stayed behind, their backs pressed against a stack of crates as they waited. The silence was deafening, every second stretching into an eternity.

Finally, Grayson's voice crackled over the radio. Shipment's confirmed. East lot. You're clear to blow it.

Nate glanced at Mara, his expression grim. Stay close.

They made their way to the east lot, where rows of trucks were lined up, their trailers packed with crates. Nate handed Mara the detonator, his eyes meeting hers.

You do it, he said softly.

What? Her hands shook as she stared at the device.

You said you wanted to help, he said. This is your chance.

Mara hesitated, the weight of the detonator pressing against her palm. She looked at Nate, at the determination in his eyes, and nodded.

Her thumb pressed down on the button.

The explosion rocked the yard, flames engulfing the trucks as a wave of heat washed over them. Alarms blared, and shouts filled the air as workers and guards scrambled to contain the chaos. Mara's heart pounded as she watched the destruction, a strange mix of fear and exhilaration surging through her.

Time to go! Nate shouted, grabbing her hand.

They ran through the maze of containers, the chaos behind them fading as they reached the tunnel. Grayson was already there, his face lit with a triumphant grin.

Hell of a show, he said. They'll be feeling that one for a while.

Mara glanced back at the yard, the flames casting long shadows against the night sky. For the first time, she felt like they'd gained a sliver of control—a small victory in an impossible war.

But as they disappeared into the tunnel, she couldn't shake the feeling that the retaliation would be swift—and merciless.

19

The Fallout

The tunnel felt like a sanctuary as they trudged back toward the forest, their boots splashing through the shallow, stagnant water. Mara's ears still rang from the explosion, her body humming with adrenaline. She could feel Nate's steady presence behind her, his breathing calm despite the chaos they'd left behind.

Not bad for a rookie, Grayson said, glancing over his shoulder at her. His grin was wide, but his eyes held an edge of respect. You've got guts, sweetheart. I'll give you that.

Mara ignored the nickname, her focus on placing one foot in front of the other. The weight of what they'd just done pressed heavily on her chest. She'd pushed the detonator; she'd sent the flames roaring through the yard. And while the destruction had felt like a win, the guilt of what might come next gnawed at her.

What happens now? she asked, her voice echoing in the narrow space.

They'll retaliate, Nate said bluntly. And fast.

Westwood's right, Grayson added. We just kicked the hornet's nest. They'll throw everything they've got into hunting us down.

Great, Mara muttered. That's comforting.

Grayson chuckled, but Nate didn't respond. His silence was more unnerving than the thought of their pursuers.

The farmhouse came into view just as dawn began to break, the sky painted in muted shades of orange and gray. The exhaustion hit Mara all at once, her legs threatening to give out as they climbed the porch steps. Inside, the familiar creak of the floorboards greeted them, but the sense of safety the house had once offered was gone.

Grayson disappeared into the kitchen, muttering something about coffee, while Nate moved toward the dining table, his expression grim. Mara lingered in the doorway, her fingers brushing against the edge of her holster.

You think they'll find us here? she asked quietly.

Eventually, Nate replied, not looking up. But not yet. We've got some time.

Time for what?

To plan our next move, he said, his tone flat. We can't let up now. If we give them room to recover, we lose the advantage.

Mara frowned, her frustration bubbling to the surface. Do you ever stop? Do you ever think about anything other than the next fight?

Nate's gaze snapped to hers, his blue eyes sharp. Every second of every day. But thinking about it doesn't change anything. This isn't over, Mara. Not until we finish it.

She held his gaze for a moment before sighing and sinking into a chair. And what if we can't finish it? What if we're just running until they catch us?

They won't, Nate said, his voice firm. Not if we stay ahead of them.

Grayson reappeared, a steaming mug in each hand. He placed one in front of Mara and the other in front of Nate before pulling out a chair for himself. As much as I love this motivational speech, we've got bigger problems.

Mara raised an eyebrow. Bigger than being hunted by a criminal network?

Grayson leaned back, his expression serious. The explosion won't go unnoticed. They'll be looking for answers, and it won't take long for them to start connecting the dots. If we don't hit them again soon, we're dead in the water.

Do you have a target in mind? Nate asked.

Grayson smirked. Always.

The next few hours passed in a blur of planning and preparation. Grayson laid out the details of their next strike—a communications hub located in the heart of the city. Disrupting it would cripple the network's ability to coordinate, buying them precious time.

This one's going to be trickier, Grayson said, his finger tracing a map. High security, plenty of eyes. But if we can get inside and take out their servers, it'll set them back weeks.

And if we get caught? Mara asked, her stomach twisting at the thought.

Then we don't, Grayson replied with a wink. Simple as that.

Nate didn't laugh. He studied the map in silence, his focus unwavering. Mara could see the tension in his shoulders, the weight of every decision pressing down on him. She wanted to reach out, to say something that might ease the burden, but the words wouldn't come.

That night, as they geared up for the mission, Mara found herself alone with Nate in the living room. He was adjusting the straps on his holster, his movements precise and practiced.

Nate, she said softly, stepping closer. Are we really making a difference? Or are we just... surviving?

He paused, his hands stilling as he looked at her. For a moment, the mask of control slipped, and she saw the exhaustion in his eyes.

We're doing both, he admitted. But surviving isn't enough. If we don't take them down, they'll keep coming. They'll destroy everything in their path.

Mara nodded, though the knot in her stomach didn't ease. And what happens when it's over? What happens to us?

His gaze held hers, the silence stretching between them like a thread on the verge of snapping. One thing at a time, Mara. Let's make it through tonight first.

She wanted to press him, to demand answers, but the sound of Grayson clearing his throat from the doorway cut her off.

Lovebirds, we're burning moonlight, he said with a grin. Let's move.

The city was a stark contrast to the forest, its streets alive with the hum of neon lights and late-night traffic. Grayson parked the truck in a shadowed alley, the towering glass and steel of the communications hub looming ahead.

This is it, Grayson said, his voice low. In and out, clean and quick. Let's make some noise.

Mara followed Nate and Grayson as they approached the building, her nerves fraying with every step. The air felt charged, the anticipation crackling like static electricity. She clutched her gun tightly, her knuckles white against the cold metal.

Inside, the hum of servers and fluorescent lights filled the air. The plan was simple: Grayson would plant the virus, Nate would handle the guards, and Mara would keep watch. But as they moved deeper into the building, the simplicity of the plan began to crumble.

A distant shout echoed down the hallway, followed by the unmistakable sound of boots on tile.

They know we're here, Nate said, his voice sharp. Move!

Mara's heart raced as they sprinted toward the server room, the sound of pursuit growing louder. The mission had just begun, but already, everything was falling apart.

20

The Fractured Mission

The sound of boots echoed ominously down the sterile hallway, each step a countdown to disaster. Mara's heart pounded as she clutched her gun, her eyes darting to Nate, who motioned for her to follow. Grayson was ahead of them, his expression grim as he pulled out the virus drive from his jacket pocket.

Server room's just down there, Grayson said, his voice low but tense. We get in, plug this thing in, and get out before they figure out what hit them.

They've already figured it out, Nate replied sharply, his eyes scanning the hallway. We're running out of time.

They reached the server room, a glass-walled enclosure filled with blinking lights and humming towers. Grayson wasted no time, stepping inside and moving toward the main console. Nate followed, his gun drawn, while Mara lingered near the doorway, her pulse racing.

Keep watch, Nate said, his voice firm.

Mara nodded, positioning herself by the door. The hallway stretched before her like an endless tunnel, the overhead lights casting harsh shadows against the white walls. Every creak, every distant murmur felt amplified, her nerves wound tighter with each passing second.

Inside the room, Grayson muttered curses under his breath as he worked to bypass the system's security. Nate stood beside him, his stance tense and ready, the weight of his protection falling silently on Mara's shoulders.

The first guard appeared so suddenly that Mara almost didn't react. He rounded the corner at the end of the hall, his flashlight cutting through the shadows. She froze for a heartbeat before instinct took over, raising her gun.

Hey! the guard barked, his voice echoing. He reached for his radio, but Mara fired before he could speak into it. The shot rang out, startlingly loud in the enclosed space. The guard crumpled to the floor, his flashlight rolling out of his hand.

Mara's breaths came in shallow gasps as she stared at the body. She'd fired without thinking, her body acting faster than her mind. The weight of what she'd just done threatened to crush her, but there was no time to process it.

More footsteps echoed down the hallway—multiple sets this time.

Nate! she hissed. We've got company.

Nate appeared at her side in an instant, his gaze sharp as he glanced down the hallway. He grabbed her arm, pulling her back into the server room just as a barrage of gunfire erupted, bullets shattering the glass wall.

Grayson, how much longer? Nate shouted over the chaos.

Almost there! Grayson yelled back, his fingers flying over the keyboard. Just keep them off me!

Mara crouched behind one of the server towers, her heart hammering in her chest. The air was thick with the acrid smell of smoke and the high-pitched whine of alarms blaring. Nate fired back at the advancing guards, his movements precise and controlled, but the sheer number of them was overwhelming.

We can't hold them off forever, Mara said, her voice trembling.

We don't have to, Nate replied. Just long enough.

Grayson let out a triumphant laugh. Done! Virus is in. Let's blow this place.

Time to move! Nate ordered, grabbing Mara's arm and pulling her toward the exit.

They sprinted down the hallway, the guards hot on their heels. The gunfire was relentless, bullets ricocheting off walls and sending shards of glass and tile flying. Mara's lungs burned as she ran, her legs threatening to give out with every step.

The stairwell loomed ahead, their one chance at escape. Nate kicked the door open, and they barreled through, the heavy metal slamming shut behind them.

Keep going! Nate shouted. We're almost there.

The sound of pursuit was deafening, the guards pounding up the stairs behind them. Grayson was the first to reach the exit at the bottom, his hand on the door handle.

But when he pushed it open, he froze.

Damn it, he muttered.

Mara skidded to a stop beside him, her stomach dropping at the sight before them. More guards stood outside, their guns trained on the door. They were surrounded.

Nate! Grayson shouted. We've got a problem.

Nate reached them, his face darkening as he took in the scene. He raised his gun, his gaze flicking between the guards outside and the ones closing in behind them.

We're not going out like this, Nate said, his voice cold. He turned to Grayson. You've got a plan?

Grayson smirked, though it didn't reach his eyes. I always do.

He pulled a grenade from his vest and held it up, his grin widening at the startled looks on the guards' faces.

You might want to duck, he said.

Grayson hurled the grenade toward the group outside, and chaos erupted. The explosion shook the building, the blast sending guards scattering as smoke and debris filled the air.

Go! Nate barked, shoving Mara forward.

They burst through the smoke, firing at the remaining guards as they sprinted toward the truck parked in the shadows. Mara could barely see through the haze, her body moving on pure adrenaline. She could hear Nate and Grayson shouting behind her, their voices muffled by the ringing in her ears.

By the time they reached the truck and peeled away from the scene, Mara's entire body was trembling. She sat in the back seat, her head resting against the window as she tried to catch her breath. Nate and Grayson were in the front, their voices low as they discussed the mission.

Virus worked, Grayson said. They'll be scrambling to rebuild their comms for weeks.

But they know we're serious now, Nate replied. The heat's only going to get worse.

Mara closed her eyes, the weight of the night pressing down on her like a physical force. They'd succeeded, but at what cost? The image of the guard she'd shot was burned into her mind, his face haunting her every thought.

She opened her eyes and looked at Nate. What now?

He met her gaze, his expression unreadable. Now we keep fighting.

21

The Enemy Tightens the Noose

The truck tore down the highway, its engine roaring against the wind. Mara sat silently in the back seat, her hands trembling in her lap. The adrenaline that had propelled her through the chaos of the mission had faded, leaving behind a bone-deep exhaustion and a pit of unease in her stomach.

Grayson adjusted the rearview mirror, catching her pale reflection. You alright back there, sweetheart?

Stop calling me that, she snapped, her voice sharper than she intended. And no, I'm not alright.

Grayson let out a low chuckle, but there was no humor in it. Welcome to the club.

Enough, Nate said from the passenger seat, his tone cutting through the tension. He glanced back at Mara, his blue eyes softer than usual. We'll debrief when we get to the safe house. Just hold on a little longer.

Safe house? Mara asked, her voice laced with skepticism. Is anywhere really safe?

It's secure, Nate said firmly, though the set of his jaw suggested even he had his doubts.

The safe house was a decrepit motel on the outskirts of a dying town, its neon vacancy sign flickering weakly against the night sky. Grayson parked the truck in a darkened corner of the lot, and the three of them climbed out, their movements heavy with fatigue.

Inside, the room smelled faintly of mildew and old smoke. The furniture was mismatched and stained, the walls decorated with faded wallpaper that peeled at the edges. Mara dropped onto the edge of the bed, her head in her hands.

Grayson tossed his bag onto a chair and stretched, his shoulders cracking. Not exactly five-star accommodations, but it'll do.

Nate didn't respond. He was already at the window, peering through the gap in the curtains. His body was taut with tension, every muscle coiled like a spring.

They'll regroup fast, he said. The explosion bought us time, but not much. We need to stay ahead of them.

Mara looked up, her exhaustion giving way to frustration. And how exactly do we do that? We've been running since this started, Nate. How do we win?

Nate turned to her, his gaze steady. We keep fighting. We find their next weak spot and hit it. Harder than before.

Grayson pulled a bottle of whiskey from his bag, unscrewing the cap with a flourish. Bold strategy. Let's hope they don't decide to hit back harder first.

They will, Nate said grimly. It's only a matter of time.

The retaliation came faster than any of them expected.

Mara had just started to drift off, her body finally succumbing to exhaustion, when the sound of shattering glass jolted her awake. She sat up, her heart racing as she registered the chaos erupting around her.

Nate! she screamed, scrambling to her feet.

Get down! he shouted, pulling her to the floor just as a bullet tore through the air above them.

Grayson was already firing back, his gun barking in rapid succession. The room was a cacophony of gunfire and shouted orders, the walls splintering as bullets tore through the flimsy structure.

Mara crawled toward the overturned dresser, her hands fumbling for the gun Nate had given her. She clutched it tightly, her breath coming in short gasps as she peeked over the edge.

The attackers were outside, their silhouettes visible through the broken window. She counted at least four, their movements coordinated and precise. They weren't amateurs.

They're flanking us! Grayson shouted, reloading his weapon.

Nate cursed under his breath, his mind racing. Mara, stay here. Don't move unless I tell you.

She nodded, her fingers trembling as she gripped the gun. Her pulse thundered in her ears, but she forced herself to focus. This wasn't the time to panic.

Nate and Grayson moved as a unit, their familiarity with this kind of situation evident in the way they covered each other. Mara watched as they returned fire, their shots deliberate and controlled.

But the attackers kept coming.

The fight spilled into the parking lot, the night lit by flashes of gunfire and the orange glow of a burning car. Mara crouched behind the truck, her breath hitching as she watched Nate and Grayson battle the relentless assault.

Her stomach twisted when she saw one of the attackers break off, circling toward her position. He moved silently, his gun raised as he scanned the shadows.

Mara's fingers tightened on her weapon. She didn't want to do this. She didn't want to take another life. But if she didn't, she knew what would happen.

As the man stepped closer, she took a deep breath and aimed. Her hands shook, but she forced herself to steady them. She waited until he was within range, then pulled the trigger.

The shot was deafening, the recoil jolting her arm. The man stumbled, clutching his chest before collapsing to the ground. Mara stared at him, her vision blurring as her mind screamed at her to look away.

Mara! Nate's voice broke through her haze. Move!

She snapped back to reality, scrambling toward him as he covered her retreat. Together, they ducked behind a stack of crates near the motel's entrance, their breaths coming in ragged gasps.

Are you okay? Nate asked, his voice urgent.

She nodded, though her hands still trembled. I… I think so.

He placed a hand on her shoulder, his grip firm and reassuring. You did good. Stay with me.

Grayson joined them moments later, his face streaked with dirt and sweat. We're clear—for now.

For now isn't good enough, Nate muttered. He glanced at Mara, his expression softening. We need to move. Can you handle it?

Yes, she said, her voice steadier than she felt. Let's go.

As they drove away from the motel, the adrenaline began to fade, leaving Mara drained and hollow. She stared out the window, the landscape blurring into a smear of darkness and faint starlight.

We can't keep doing this, she said softly. Running, fighting… it's never-ending.

Nate glanced at her, his expression unreadable. It'll end when we end it. Not before.

And how do we do that? she asked, her voice trembling. How do we stop something this big?

Grayson chuckled darkly. One piece at a time. That's how you take down a giant.

Mara didn't respond. She wasn't sure she believed them anymore. But as the truck sped into the night, she realized she didn't have a choice. They were in this together, for better or worse.

And she wouldn't let them face it alone.

22

A Line in the Sand

The morning light revealed the aftermath of the battle. The truck's windshield bore a web of cracks from stray bullets, the side panels riddled with dents and holes. Grayson swore under his breath as he guided them down a back road lined with dense trees. Every bump in the road jolted Mara, but she didn't complain. She was too tired to speak, too consumed by the images replaying in her mind—the sound of gunfire, the face of the man she'd shot, the way his body crumpled to the ground.

We can't keep going like this, she said finally, her voice barely above a whisper.

We're not, Nate said from the passenger seat, his tone sharper than she expected. We're ending it.

Grayson raised an eyebrow but kept his eyes on the road. And how exactly do you plan to do that, Westwood? We've been poking the hornet's nest, but they're still swarming.

Nate pulled out the ledger, flipping through its pages with grim determination. Because we've been playing defense. It's time to take the fight to them.

They pulled into a clearing deep in the forest, a dilapidated hunting cabin standing at its center. Grayson cut the engine and climbed out, muttering something about how much he hated the woods. Nate stepped out next, clutching the ledger like a lifeline. Mara hesitated before following, the cool air biting at her skin as she took in the isolated surroundings.

Inside, the cabin was sparse—just a couple of chairs, a wood-burning stove, and a table covered in old hunting magazines. Grayson began checking the windows while Nate spread the ledger across the table, his focus unwavering.

What's the plan? Mara asked, sinking into one of the chairs.

Nate glanced at her, his blue eyes alight with something she hadn't seen before: resolve. We stop running. We stop reacting. We dismantle the network from the inside out.

And how do we do that? she pressed.

By turning their own people against them, Nate said. He tapped a name circled in the ledger. David Kline. Mid-level enforcer, handles recruitment. He's greedy, and he's had issues with the higher-ups before. If we can get him to flip, he could give us access to their internal communications.

Mara frowned. And if he doesn't flip?

Then we make sure he can't hurt us, Nate replied, his tone cold. One way or another.

Grayson chuckled darkly. I like this new version of you, Westwood. Ruthless suits you.

It's not about being ruthless, Nate said, his gaze hard. It's about survival.

The plan to intercept David Kline was simple on paper: ambush him at one of his favorite haunts—a seedy bar known for its lack of questions and abundance of danger. Grayson had done the reconnaissance, and Nate had sketched out the details. Mara's role was clear: stay close, stay quiet, and only act if necessary.

The bar reeked of stale beer and cigarette smoke, its patrons a mix of surly regulars and shadowy figures who clearly had something to hide. Mara followed Nate inside, her heart pounding as her eyes scanned the room. Grayson had taken a position outside, watching the exits.

There, Nate murmured, nodding toward a booth in the back corner.

David Kline was hard to miss. He was large, with a thick neck and hands that looked like they could crush bone. He sat with his back to the wall, a half-empty glass of whiskey in front of him. His eyes were sharp, darting around the room like a predator sizing up prey.

Nate approached first, his movements calm and deliberate. Mara trailed behind, every muscle in her body taut with tension.

Kline, Nate said, sliding into the booth across from him. We need to talk.

Kline's lips curled into a sneer. Westwood. I heard you were still breathing. Figured that wouldn't last long.

That depends on you, Nate replied evenly. We've got a problem. And you're the solution.

Kline snorted, leaning back in his seat. You've got guts, I'll give you that. But I don't solve problems for free.

Nate slid a USB drive across the table. This is a small taste of what I've got—financial records tying the network to some very powerful people. You help us, and I make sure your name stays out of it.

Kline picked up the drive, turning it over in his hand. And if I don't?

Then your name goes straight to the authorities, Nate said, his tone hardening. And trust me, I've got more than enough to make sure you go down with them.

Mara's breath caught as Kline's eyes narrowed. For a moment, she thought he might lash out, but then he laughed—a low, guttural sound that sent a chill down her spine.

You've changed, Westwood, he said, pocketing the drive. Fine. I'll help. But if you screw me over, you won't live to regret it.

Nate nodded, standing. Deal.

They left the bar quickly, disappearing into the night before Kline could change his mind. Grayson was waiting in the truck, his arms crossed.

Well? he asked as they climbed in.

He's in, Nate said.

For now, Mara added, her voice quiet.

Grayson smirked. That's all we need.

Back at the cabin, the tension was palpable. The deal with Kline felt like progress, but the weight of what lay ahead loomed large. Mara sat by the window, staring out at the dark forest as Nate poured over the ledger.

You okay? he asked, joining her.

She shook her head. Not really.

Nate leaned against the windowsill, his expression softening. I know this is hard, Mara. But we're getting closer. Every step we take, we're hitting them where it hurts.

And what happens when they hit back? she asked, her voice trembling. How do we keep going?

Nate reached out, his hand brushing hers. We just do. Because if we don't, no one else will.

Mara looked at him, her fear warring with the faintest spark of hope. She didn't know if they could win, but as long as Nate was beside her, she knew she'd keep fighting.

And maybe—just maybe—that would be enough.

23

The Fragile Alliance

The forest surrounding the cabin was silent, the air heavy with the weight of an impending storm. Inside, the tension was just as oppressive. Mara sat at the table, her fingers idly tracing the grain of the wood as Nate and Grayson went over the next steps. The deal with David Kline had gone smoother than expected, but the victory felt hollow, like a matchstick shielding them from an avalanche.

Kline's information checks out, Grayson said, holding up a tablet that displayed a list of names and locations. He's giving us access to their comms hub. If we can get inside, we'll have the whole network's communications at our fingertips.

And what's the catch? Mara asked, unable to hide her skepticism.

Grayson smirked. The catch is it's heavily guarded, and once we're in, we'll have a small window to download everything before they figure out what's happening.

How small? Nate asked, his voice steady but grim.

Ten minutes, tops, Grayson replied. If we're lucky.

Mara shook her head, her stomach twisting. This sounds impossible.

Most good plans do, Grayson said with a shrug. But this is the best shot we've got.

Nate leaned forward, his gaze fixed on the map spread across the table. We'll need a diversion. Something big enough to draw their attention away from the hub.

I can handle that, Grayson said, a grin tugging at his lips. Explosions are kind of my specialty.

Mara crossed her arms. And what about us? What do we do while you're blowing things up?

You and Nate get inside, Grayson said. You're the tech wizard, right? You handle the download. Nate handles anyone who gets too close.

Mara frowned. I wouldn't call myself a wizard.

Well, then I hope you're a fast learner, Grayson said with a wink. Because this is happening tomorrow night.

The hours leading up to the mission were a blur of preparation. Nate and Grayson checked their weapons and gear, their movements efficient and methodical. Mara felt like a bystander, her nerves fraying with every passing moment. She tried to focus on the task ahead, but the weight of what they were about to do pressed heavily on her.

Hey, Nate said, his voice breaking through her spiraling thoughts. He crouched beside her, his blue eyes soft. You've got this.

She forced a smile, though it didn't reach her eyes. I don't feel like I do.

You don't have to feel it, he said gently. You just have to do it.

Mara nodded, the knot in her stomach loosening slightly. Nate's confidence in her was a strange kind of anchor, steadying her in the chaos.

The comms hub was a sprawling facility on the edge of the city, its perimeter guarded by high fences and security cameras. Grayson dropped them off a few blocks away, the rumble of his truck fading into the night as he disappeared to set the diversion.

Stay close, Nate said, his voice low.

Mara followed him through the shadows, her heart pounding as they approached the fence. The sound of their breathing was the only thing cutting through the stillness. Nate crouched by the fence, cutting through the links with a pair of wire cutters. The metal groaned softly, and Mara winced, half-expecting alarms to blare.

But none came.

They slipped through the gap and moved toward the building, sticking to the shadows. The faint hum of generators filled the air, mingling with the distant murmur of voices from the guards patrolling the perimeter.

Nate held up a hand, signaling for her to stop. He pointed to a vent near the base of the building, its grating held in place by a few rusted screws.

In there, he whispered. It'll take us to the server room.

Mara nodded, crawling into the vent as Nate unscrewed the grating. The metal was cold against her hands and knees, the narrow space forcing her to move slowly. She tried to focus on the task at hand, but her mind kept drifting to what might happen if they were caught.

When they reached the end of the vent, Nate pushed the next grating open and dropped into the server room. Mara followed, her breath catching as she took in the rows of servers humming softly in the dim light.

This is it, Nate said, pulling a USB drive from his pocket. Plug this into the main terminal. It'll start the download automatically.

Mara's fingers trembled as she took the drive and approached the terminal. The screen glowed faintly, its interface unfamiliar but intuitive enough. She plugged in the drive, her breath hitching as the download bar appeared.

Ten minutes, she said, her voice barely above a whisper.

Nate nodded, positioning himself by the door. We just have to hold out until then.

The first sign of trouble came sooner than they'd expected. The distant sound of an explosion shook the building, followed by the blaring of alarms. Mara's heart raced as the red lights of the emergency system bathed the room in an ominous glow.

That's Grayson's diversion, Nate said, his gun raised. Stay focused.

Mara stared at the download bar, willing it to move faster. The percentage ticked up agonizingly slowly, each second stretching into an eternity.

Footsteps echoed in the hallway outside, and Mara's stomach dropped. Nate tensed, his finger hovering over the trigger.

The door burst open, and two guards stormed in. Nate fired before they could react, his shots precise and deadly. Mara flinched at the sound, her focus breaking for a moment before she forced herself back to the screen.

Almost there, she said, her voice shaking.

More footsteps. More gunfire. Nate moved like a predator, his movements efficient and controlled as he took down one guard after another. Mara could see the strain in his eyes, the way his jaw clenched with every shot.

The download bar finally reached 100%, and Mara pulled the USB drive free, clutching it tightly in her hand. Got it!

Move! Nate shouted, grabbing her arm.

They sprinted toward the vent, the sound of pursuit close behind. Mara's lungs burned as she crawled through the narrow space, Nate's urgency propelling her forward. When they emerged outside, the night was alive with chaos—flames and smoke billowed from the far side of the facility, Grayson's handiwork evident.

The truck screeched to a halt nearby, Grayson leaning out of the driver's side window. Get in!

Mara and Nate dove into the back seat as bullets ricocheted off the truck's exterior. Grayson floored the gas pedal, the tires screeching as they sped away from the comms hub.

Back at the cabin, the USB drive sat on the table like a trophy. Mara stared at it, her body still trembling from the adrenaline. Nate and Grayson were debriefing, their voices low, but she couldn't focus on their words.

We did it, Nate said finally, turning to her. We've got their comms. This is the break we needed.

Mara nodded, though her mind was already racing ahead. They'd won a battle, but the war was far from over.

And the enemy was still out there, waiting to strike.

24

The Enemy Strikes Back

The tension in the cabin was palpable as Nate and Grayson pored over the data from the USB drive. Mara sat on the edge of the couch, her fingers curled around a mug of lukewarm coffee. Her exhaustion was bone-deep, but her mind wouldn't quiet. The weight of the mission's success felt overshadowed by the knowledge that their enemies wouldn't let this slide.

They're using coded messages, Nate muttered, scrolling through the data on his laptop. Encrypted comms. It's going to take time to crack.

Grayson leaned back in his chair, his arms crossed. Time we don't have. They'll be scrambling to plug the holes we just blew in their operation.

They'll come for us, Mara said, her voice quiet but steady. They won't just sit back and wait.

They're already looking, Nate said grimly, his eyes scanning the screen. They've flagged us as high-priority targets. If they didn't know where we were before, they'll figure it out soon.

Grayson smirked, though there was no humor in it. Let them come. We've got enough firepower to make them regret it.

It's not just about firepower, Nate said sharply. It's about strategy. We need to stay ahead of them.

And what's your brilliant strategy? Grayson asked.

Nate's jaw tightened. We take out their leadership.

The room fell silent, the weight of Nate's words settling over them like a storm cloud. Mara's stomach twisted as she processed what he was saying.

You mean...? she began, her voice trailing off.

We cut the head off the snake, Nate said, his tone cold and resolute. We've been dismantling their operation piece by piece, but if we take out their leaders, the entire network will collapse.

Grayson let out a low whistle. Bold move, Westwood. You got names?

Nate nodded, his eyes flicking back to the laptop. There are three key players: Marcus Hargrove, Eleanor Pierce, and Victor Shaw. Hargrove handles logistics, Pierce controls finances, and Shaw... he's the enforcer. The muscle. We take them down, and the rest will crumble.

And how exactly do we do that? Mara asked, her voice trembling slightly. These people don't exactly leave themselves exposed.

We divide and conquer, Nate said. Hargrove's already on shaky ground after the warehouse hit. He'll be vulnerable. Pierce operates out of a high-rise downtown—hard to reach, but not impossible. And Shaw... he's dangerous, but he's predictable. He always comes after blood.

Grayson chuckled darkly. Sounds like a fun challenge.

Mara stared at Nate, her heart pounding. You really think this will work?

It has to, he said simply.

They decided to start with Marcus Hargrove. According to the intel from the USB drive, he'd relocated his operations to a storage facility on the outskirts of the city. It was a temporary setup, hastily constructed in the aftermath of the warehouse explosion. Nate's plan was straightforward: infiltrate, isolate, and eliminate.

The drive to the facility was tense, the silence in the truck broken only by the faint hum of the engine. Mara clutched her gun tightly, her palms damp with sweat. She'd faced danger before, but this felt different. They weren't just defending themselves—they were going on the offensive.

You ready for this? Nate asked, his voice cutting through the quiet.

No, she admitted. But I'll do it anyway.

He gave her a faint smile. That's all that matters.

The storage facility was a maze of shipping containers and makeshift offices, its perimeter patrolled by armed guards. Nate led the way, his movements silent and deliberate as they slipped through the shadows. Grayson brought up the rear, his expression unusually serious.

When they reached the edge of the main building, Nate held up a hand, signaling for them to stop. He pointed to a window on the second floor, its curtains drawn but faint light spilling through the edges.

Hargrove's in there, Nate whispered. We get in, cut off his comms, and take him out.

Grayson nodded, already pulling out a set of tools to disable the lock on the side entrance. Mara's heart raced as they moved inside, the air heavy with the faint smell of oil and dust.

The building was eerily quiet, the distant murmur of voices their only clue that they weren't alone. Nate led them up a metal staircase, each step creaking under their weight. Mara's grip on her gun tightened as they approached the door to Hargrove's office.

Nate signaled for Grayson to take point, his movements precise and practiced. Grayson slipped a small device from his pocket and pressed it against the lock. The light on the device blinked green, and the door clicked open.

The office was sparse, its walls lined with maps and whiteboards covered in scribbled notes. Marcus Hargrove sat at a desk, his back to them, a phone pressed to his ear.

We lost the shipment, and the comms hub is down, Hargrove was saying, his voice tense. We need—

He turned, his eyes widening as he saw them. Before he could react, Nate fired, the silenced shot hitting its mark. Hargrove slumped in his chair, his phone clattering to the floor.

Clean, Grayson said, a hint of admiration in his voice. Nice work, Westwood.

Mara stared at Hargrove's lifeless body, her stomach churning. She'd known what they were here to do, but seeing it play out felt surreal.

We need to move, Nate said, his voice cutting through her thoughts. He grabbed a stack of papers from the desk and shoved them into his bag. They'll know something's wrong soon.

The escape was chaotic. The guards discovered them as they reached the ground floor, their shouts echoing through the building. Grayson lobbed a smoke grenade, the thick cloud giving them just enough cover to reach the exit.

Mara's lungs burned as they sprinted through the maze of containers, bullets ricocheting off the metal around them. She could hear Nate shouting behind her, but his words were drowned out by the chaos.

When they finally reached the truck, Grayson floored the gas pedal, the tires screeching as they sped away. Mara collapsed against the seat, her chest heaving as she tried to catch her breath.

One down, Nate said, his voice steady despite the tension. Two to go.

Mara glanced at him, her pulse still racing. And then what?

Then we end this, he said, his gaze hard. For good.

25

A Quiet Fury

The truck roared through the countryside, the engine's steady hum a sharp contrast to the storm brewing inside Mara. She sat in the back seat, her hands clasped tightly in her lap as she tried to steady her breathing. The image of Marcus Hargrove's lifeless body wouldn't leave her mind, replaying over and over like a haunting melody.

Grayson broke the silence, his tone almost cheerful. Well, that was a hell of a show. One less scumbag in the world.

Mara snapped her head toward him, her voice trembling with barely contained anger. He wasn't just a 'scumbag,' Grayson. He was a person.

Grayson arched an eyebrow, glancing at her in the rearview mirror. A person who would've killed us without blinking. Don't get soft on me now, sweetheart.

Don't call me that, she said sharply, her voice rising. And don't act like this is some kind of game. People are dying.

Grayson's grin faded, his tone turning serious. Yeah, they are. And unless we keep doing what we're doing, more people will. You think I like this?

That I enjoy it? Newsflash: none of us do. But we don't have the luxury of second-guessing every move.

Enough, Nate said from the passenger seat, his voice cutting through the tension like a blade. He turned to look at Mara, his blue eyes softening. He's right about one thing, Mara. This isn't easy. But it's necessary.

Mara shook her head, her frustration bubbling over. And when does it stop, Nate? When do we stop justifying this? When do we stop turning into them?

It stops when they're gone, he said simply.

The words hung in the air, heavy and unyielding. Mara turned away, staring out the window as the countryside blurred into a smear of green and gray.

The next target was Eleanor Pierce, the network's financial mastermind. According to the intel Nate had pulled from Hargrove's office, Pierce operated out of a high-rise in the heart of the city, her wealth and influence shielding her from the chaos brewing below. She was the network's lifeline, the one who kept their operations afloat with her connections and financial acumen.

We take her out, and we cut off their funding, Nate said, his tone clipped as he spread a map across the table in their temporary safe house. But this one's not going to be easy. She's got private security, surveillance, and enough pull to make people disappear.

Grayson let out a low whistle. Sounds like my kind of party.

Mara frowned, her stomach twisting with unease. And how exactly are we supposed to get close to her?

With this, Nate said, sliding a small device across the table. It looked like a sleek black credit card, but Mara recognized it as a high-tech access tool—a hacker's dream.

What is it? she asked.

Key card mimic, Nate explained. It can clone any card with an RFID chip. We just need to get close enough to her or one of her staff to copy their credentials.

And once we're inside? Grayson asked.

We make it look like an accident, Nate said. No fireworks this time. Subtle. Clean.

Mara's stomach churned. You make it sound so simple.

It's not, Nate admitted, his gaze locking with hers. But we don't have a choice.

They parked a few blocks from the high-rise, the bustling city around them a stark contrast to the quiet tension inside the truck. Nate and Mara would handle the infiltration while Grayson stayed outside, monitoring the building's security feeds through a portable rig.

Stay sharp, Grayson said as Nate and Mara climbed out. And don't do anything I wouldn't do.

Mara rolled her eyes, but her heart wasn't in it. Her nerves were stretched taut as she followed Nate through the crowd, their target looming ahead like a glass-and-steel fortress. The lobby was sleek and modern, its polished floors gleaming under the bright overhead lights.

She'll be in her office on the top floor, Nate murmured as they approached the security desk. Keep your head down.

Mara nodded, her pulse quickening as they passed the guards. Nate's confidence was a shield, his calm demeanor helping her mask the storm raging inside her. They slipped into the elevator without incident, the doors closing with a soft chime.

Nate pulled out the key card mimic, holding it against the elevator's control panel. The device beeped softly, the display lighting up with a new set of options.

Penthouse, he said, pressing the button.

Mara clenched her fists, her nerves fraying with every second. What happens if someone catches us?

They won't, Nate said, his voice steady. Just stick to the plan.

The elevator doors opened into a lavish office suite, its floor-to-ceiling windows offering a breathtaking view of the city. Eleanor Pierce sat at a massive desk, her back to them as she typed on a sleek laptop. She didn't even look up as they entered.

Nate moved first, his steps silent as he approached. Mara followed, her heart hammering in her chest. She could feel the tension radiating off Nate, the weight of what they were about to do pressing down on both of them.

Pierce finally looked up, her sharp green eyes narrowing as she took them in. You're not supposed to be here.

No, Nate said, his voice cold. But you knew we'd come eventually.

Pierce's expression didn't waver. You think killing me will stop the network? You're more naïve than I thought.

It's not about stopping it, Nate said. It's about cutting the roots so it can't grow back.

Pierce laughed, the sound brittle and hollow. You don't understand how deep this goes.

Then enlighten us, Nate said, his gun steady in his hand.

Pierce's gaze flicked to Mara, her lips curving into a faint smirk. Does he tell you everything? Or just enough to keep you on his side?

Mara's stomach twisted. What are you talking about?

Pierce's smirk widened. You'll find out soon enough.

Nate didn't give her a chance to say more. The shot was quick, efficient, and final. Pierce slumped forward, her blood pooling on the pristine white desk.

Mara turned away, bile rising in her throat. She stumbled toward the elevator, the weight of what they'd done crashing down on her like a tidal wave. Nate followed, his face a mask of resolve, but she could see the cracks forming beneath the surface.

Let's go, he said quietly.

Back in the truck, the tension was suffocating. Grayson didn't say anything, his usual sarcasm absent as he started the engine and pulled into traffic.

Mara stared out the window, her hands trembling in her lap. She could still hear Pierce's voice, her cryptic words ringing in her ears.

What did she mean? Mara asked, her voice barely above a whisper. What aren't you telling me?

Nate didn't respond, his gaze fixed on the road ahead.

Mara, Grayson said softly, breaking the silence. Now's not the time.

No, she snapped, turning to Nate. If there's something I need to know, you'd better tell me.

Nate's jaw tightened, his knuckles white against the steering wheel. I will. But not now.

The words did little to ease her frustration. She leaned back against the seat, her mind racing with questions she wasn't sure she wanted answered.

26

The Fractured Truth

The truck's rumble filled the silence as the city lights faded behind them. Mara sat in the back seat, her arms crossed tightly over her chest, anger and confusion warring within her. Nate's refusal to answer her questions felt like a betrayal, an insult to the trust she'd placed in him despite the danger they faced together.

Grayson glanced at her in the rearview mirror, his expression unusually serious. Whatever's eating you two, you'd better deal with it. This isn't the time to fall apart.

Nobody's falling apart, Nate said sharply, his gaze fixed on the road.

Mara leaned forward, her voice laced with frustration. Then why won't you tell me what Pierce meant? If you know something that puts us all at risk, I have a right to know.

Nate's grip on the wheel tightened, his jaw working silently for a moment. Finally, he let out a long breath. Pierce was playing a game. She wanted to mess with your head.

Is that all it was? Mara pressed. Because it didn't sound like it.

Nate didn't respond, and the silence that followed was deafening.

Grayson sighed, shaking his head. You two need a counselor.

Grayson, Nate warned, his voice low.

Fine, fine, Grayson muttered. But you'd better sort this out before it blows up in our faces.

The safe house was a small, abandoned garage tucked away in a forgotten industrial park. The faint smell of oil and rust lingered in the air as they unloaded their gear. Mara stayed close to the truck, her thoughts spiraling as Nate and Grayson began setting up their equipment.

When Nate finally approached her, his expression was a mixture of guilt and resolve.

Mara, he began, his voice soft.

She turned to face him, her arms still crossed. You're hiding something. Don't deny it.

He ran a hand through his hair, his shoulders sagging. It's not what you think.

Then tell me what it is, she said, her tone sharp.

Nate hesitated, his eyes searching hers. Pierce was right about one thing: this network goes deeper than we thought. It's not just criminals running a racket. There are people in power—politicians, CEOs, law enforcement—keeping it alive.

Mara's stomach twisted. You knew this?

I suspected, Nate admitted. But I didn't have proof until now.

And you didn't tell me? Her voice rose, anger flaring. You kept this from me while we've been risking our lives?

I didn't want to scare you, Nate said, his voice tightening. I thought I could protect you.

Mara shook her head, stepping back. I don't need your protection, Nate. I need the truth.

That is the truth, he said, his voice rising. And if you'd let me finish, I'd tell you what we're going to do about it.

She stopped, her breath coming in shallow gasps. Then tell me.

Nate stepped closer, his voice dropping. Pierce wasn't just running their finances. She was paying off people in high places to keep the network hidden. And one of those people... was someone close to my father.

Mara's blood ran cold. Who?

Nate's gaze darkened. Victor Shaw.

The revelation hung in the air like a storm cloud. Mara stared at Nate, her mind racing. She remembered the name from the ledger—Victor Shaw, the network's enforcer, the one Nate had said was predictable but dangerous. She hadn't realized how personal it was for him.

He was my father's right hand, Nate said, his voice tight. The one who handled the dirty work. When my father died, Shaw was supposed to take over. But instead, he turned the network into what it is now—a machine that eats people alive.

And now he's after us, Mara said, her voice trembling.

Nate nodded. And he won't stop until we're dead.

Grayson joined them, his arms crossed as he leaned against the truck. Sounds like Shaw's our next target.

He has to be, Nate said. If we take him out, we not only cripple the network— we send a message to everyone supporting it. No one's untouchable.

Mara felt a flicker of unease. You make it sound easy. But if Shaw is as dangerous as you say, how do we even get close to him?

That's the hard part, Nate admitted. Shaw's paranoid. He moves constantly, never stays in one place for long. But we've got something he doesn't.

What's that? Grayson asked.

Nate's expression hardened. Pierce's financial records. They'll lead us to him.

The hours that followed were a blur of planning and preparation. Nate and Grayson poured over the data pulled from Pierce's office, their voices low and intense as they mapped out Shaw's movements. Mara stayed on the periphery, her mind racing with a mix of fear and determination.

She couldn't deny the growing rift between her and Nate. His secrecy, his calculated decisions—it all felt like a betrayal. But she also couldn't ignore the pull she felt toward him, the way his resolve inspired her to keep fighting.

You okay? Nate's voice broke through her thoughts.

She looked up to find him standing in front of her, his expression unreadable. I don't know, she admitted. I'm scared. And I'm angry. And I don't know if I trust you.

Nate flinched, her words cutting deep. But he didn't look away. I get it. And I don't blame you. But I need you with me, Mara. I can't do this without you.

She studied him, her heart aching. Then stop shutting me out. Stop making decisions for me.

Nate nodded, his gaze steady. I will.

For the first time in what felt like hours, she felt a sliver of hope. It wasn't enough to erase the cracks in their partnership, but it was a start.

As the night deepened, the plan began to take shape. They would use the data to track Shaw's location, infiltrate his stronghold, and take him out. It was ambitious, risky, and fraught with danger.

But it was their only chance.

As they prepared for the mission, Mara felt the weight of everything they'd been through pressing down on her. The losses, the sacrifices, the lives they'd taken—it all led to this.

And she wasn't sure if any of them would come out of it alive.

27

The Last Line

The following day dawned cold and gray, the sky heavy with clouds that mirrored the weight in Mara's chest. The garage-turned-safe-house was silent except for the occasional scrape of metal as Grayson checked their weapons. Nate sat at the table, his laptop open, his focus unwavering as he sifted through the information they'd gathered from Pierce's financial records.

Mara leaned against the wall, her arms crossed, watching the quiet flurry of preparation. The air between her and Nate was still charged, but there was an unspoken truce for now. They couldn't afford distractions—not when everything was about to come to a head.

Grayson broke the silence, his voice low but sharp. Got a hit. Shaw's holed up in a private estate about forty miles out. He's paranoid, alright—place is like a fortress.

How well guarded? Nate asked, not looking up from the laptop.

Grayson shrugged. Standard for someone like him. Armed guards, surveillance, probably a panic room. The works.

Can we get in undetected? Mara asked, stepping closer.

Grayson smirked. With the right amount of noise, we can get in anywhere.

No noise, Nate said firmly, finally looking up. We need to be in and out before they know we're there.

Grayson raised an eyebrow. You're no fun, Westwood.

This isn't about fun, Nate said, his voice cold. It's about ending this.

The drive to Shaw's estate was tense, the air inside the truck heavy with anticipation. The estate loomed ahead like a fortress carved from stone, its high walls and iron gates casting long shadows over the surrounding forest. From their vantage point on a nearby hill, Mara could see guards patrolling the perimeter, their rifles slung casually over their shoulders.

We're not walking through the front door, Grayson said, his tone dry.

No, Nate agreed, his eyes scanning the layout. There's a service entrance at the back. Less guarded, but it'll still be a tight squeeze.

What's the plan once we're inside? Mara asked, her nerves fraying at the edges.

We split up, Nate said. Grayson takes out the surveillance. Mara, you're with me. We find Shaw, corner him, and end this.

Grayson gave a mock salute. On it, boss.

Mara's stomach churned as they moved toward the estate, the shadows of the trees their only cover. Her mind raced with what-ifs, but she forced herself to focus. She couldn't afford to hesitate—not now.

The service entrance was exactly as Nate had described: a narrow gate tucked behind a row of bushes, with only one guard stationed nearby. Grayson took him out swiftly, his movements precise and silent. The guard crumpled to the ground without a sound, and they slipped through the gate, their breaths shallow and quick.

The interior of the estate was eerily quiet, the manicured gardens and stone pathways giving way to the looming bulk of the main house. Grayson veered off toward the surveillance hub, while Nate and Mara moved toward the main building.

Stay close, Nate whispered, his voice barely audible.

Mara nodded, her grip tightening on her gun as they entered through a side door. The hallway was dimly lit, the faint hum of electricity the only sound. Every step felt like a gamble, the weight of their mission pressing down on her with each passing second.

Shaw's office was on the second floor, a sprawling space lined with book-shelves and expensive artwork. The man himself sat behind a massive desk, his back to the door, the faint glow of his computer screen illuminating his silhouette.

Nate moved first, his gun steady as he stepped into the room. Victor Shaw.

Shaw turned slowly, his expression calm, almost amused. He was a tall man, his presence commanding, his gray hair neatly combed back. He leaned back in his chair, folding his hands in his lap.

Well, well, he said, his voice smooth. Nathaniel Westwood. I was wondering when you'd show up.

Mara felt a chill run down her spine as Shaw's gaze flicked to her. And who's this? Your latest protégé?

Let's skip the games, Nate said, his voice cold. You know why we're here.

Shaw smirked. I do. But let me ask you something, Nathaniel: Do you really think killing me will change anything? Do you think it'll stop the machine your father built?

It's not just about stopping it, Nate said. It's about sending a message.

Shaw laughed, the sound rich and hollow. You sound just like him, you know. Righteous. Determined. And completely blind to the bigger picture.

Mara glanced at Nate, her heart sinking at the flicker of doubt in his eyes. Shaw was trying to get under his skin, to manipulate him, but she could see the strain it was causing.

Enough, she said, stepping forward. You're done, Shaw.

Shaw's gaze shifted to her, his smirk widening. Ah, the voice of reason. Tell me, do you even know what you're fighting for? Or are you just following him blindly?

Mara's hands tightened on her gun, her anger boiling over. I know exactly what I'm fighting for. People like you don't get to destroy lives and walk away.

Shaw stood slowly, his movements deliberate. And yet, here you are. Taking lives to save lives. How noble.

Shut up, Nate snapped, his gun rising. You don't get to lecture us.

Shaw raised his hands, his smirk never wavering. Go ahead, then. Do it. But ask yourself this, Nathaniel: What happens when the dust settles? Who will you be when the killing is over?

Nate's finger hovered over the trigger, his jaw clenched. Mara could see the conflict in his eyes, the weight of everything they'd done threatening to crush him.

Nate, she said softly. Don't let him get to you.

He glanced at her, and in that moment, she saw him make his decision. His gun fired, the shot echoing through the room. Shaw staggered, his smirk fading as he collapsed to the ground.

Mara exhaled shakily, her entire body trembling. It was over. Victor Shaw was dead.

The drive back to the safe house was silent, the weight of what they'd done pressing down on all of them. Grayson was uncharacteristically quiet, his usual smirk absent as he focused on the road. Nate sat rigid in the passenger seat, his face a mask of stone.

Mara stared out the window, her thoughts a tangled mess. They'd taken down the network's enforcer, but the cost of their victory felt unbearably high.

What now? she asked quietly.

Nate didn't answer right away. When he finally spoke, his voice was barely above a whisper. We keep going.

Mara nodded, her resolve hardening. They were in too deep to stop now.

But she couldn't shake the feeling that the worst was yet to come.

28

The Cracks Beneath the Surface

The safe house was cold, the kind of chill that seeped into Mara's bones and refused to leave. She sat at the table, staring blankly at the notes and maps spread across its surface. The faint hum of the old refrigerator was the only sound in the room, a fragile normalcy against the chaos that seemed to follow them.

Victor Shaw was dead.

The realization should have brought relief, but it felt hollow. The man who had been the network's enforcer, its unyielding fist, was gone, and yet the fight was far from over.

Across the room, Nate sat in silence, his elbows resting on his knees as he stared at the floor. His usual resolve had been replaced by something quieter, darker. The weight of what they'd done, what they'd become, hung heavily between them.

Grayson leaned against the doorframe, his expression unreadable as he lit a cigarette. He exhaled a cloud of smoke, watching it curl toward the ceiling before speaking.

Well, he said, his voice breaking the silence. We've cut off the head. What's left of the beast?

Nate didn't look up. Pierce's files mentioned a fallback plan. The network isn't dead yet. Without Shaw, they'll regroup. Someone will take his place.

Grayson let out a low chuckle. Figures. Cut off one head, two more grow back. Classic hydra.

This isn't a game, Grayson, Nate snapped, his voice sharp.

Grayson raised his hands in mock surrender. Easy, Westwood. I'm on your side, remember?

Mara glanced at Nate, her frustration bubbling beneath the surface. Are you? Because it feels like we're all just following orders without knowing the full picture.

Nate finally looked at her, his eyes hard. You know as much as I do, Mara. This is bigger than all of us.

That doesn't make it easier, she shot back. We've killed people, Nate. People who probably deserved it, sure, but when does it end?

When we've finished what we started, he said simply.

Mara shook her head, standing abruptly. You say that like it's so easy. Like we're not losing pieces of ourselves every time we pull the trigger.

Nate stood too, his voice rising. You think I don't know that? You think I don't feel it?

The room fell silent, the tension crackling like a live wire. Grayson cleared his throat, stepping between them.

Alright, lovebirds, he said, his tone dry. Let's save the melodrama for later. We've still got work to do.

The next step was to track the remnants of the network. Pierce's files hinted at a final location—a secure compound deep in the mountains, where the surviving members of the leadership would regroup. It was their last bastion, their fallback plan if everything else collapsed.

Grayson spread a map across the table, tracing a route with his finger. It's a fortress. High-tech security, limited access points, and probably enough firepower to start a war.

Sounds like fun, Nate said, his tone flat.

Mara frowned, her unease growing. How do we even get close to something like that?

Grayson grinned, tapping a location on the map. With a little creativity. There's an access road here, barely used. If we take out their perimeter defenses, we might have a shot at slipping inside.

And then what? Mara asked. We go in guns blazing?

Not exactly, Nate said. We plant explosives on their infrastructure—power, communications, supply lines. We force them to scatter.

And when they scatter? she pressed.

We pick them off, he said, his gaze unwavering.

The drive to the mountains was grueling, the narrow roads winding through dense forests and jagged cliffs. The air grew colder the higher they climbed, the scent of pine and damp earth filling the truck. Mara sat in the back, her thoughts heavy as the landscape blurred past.

She couldn't shake the feeling that they were walking into a trap. The network had been one step ahead of them before—what if they were waiting? What if this was exactly what they wanted?

We'll be fine, Nate said, breaking the silence. It wasn't clear if he was talking to her or himself.

Mara met his gaze in the rearview mirror. Will we?

He didn't answer.

The compound came into view as the sun dipped below the horizon, its high walls and watchtowers silhouetted against the darkening sky. The perimeter was heavily guarded, armed men patrolling the walls while floodlights swept the surrounding forest.

Lovely place, Grayson muttered, adjusting his scope as he surveyed the defenses. Nothing like a warm welcome.

Nate crouched beside him, his face lit by the faint glow of their equipment. We disable the lights first, then the towers. Once we're inside, we stick to the plan.

Mara joined them, her stomach twisting with nerves. And if the plan goes wrong?

It won't, Nate said, his voice firm. We've come too far to fail now.

She wanted to believe him. But as they moved toward the compound, the weight of everything they'd endured pressed down on her like a storm cloud.

The first phase of the mission went smoothly. Grayson's expertise with explosives allowed them to disable the floodlights and surveillance equipment without raising an alarm. The darkness became their ally, shrouding their movements as they scaled the outer wall.

Inside, the compound was a maze of buildings and open courtyards, the faint hum of generators filling the air. Nate led the way, his gun drawn, his every movement purposeful and controlled. Mara followed close behind, her heart pounding as they approached the central building.

This is it, Nate whispered. The heart of their operation.

Grayson pulled out a small device, attaching it to the side of the building. Five minutes, he said. Then this place goes dark.

Let's make them count, Nate replied.

They moved deeper into the compound, their footsteps silent on the cold concrete. But as they reached the main hallway, Mara's instincts screamed a warning.

Wait, she whispered, grabbing Nate's arm.

Too late.

The lights snapped on, and the sound of boots echoed around them. Armed men poured into the hallway, their weapons raised, their faces cold and unyielding.

Drop your weapons! one of them barked.

Mara's heart raced as she raised her hands, her mind scrambling for a way out. Beside her, Nate's jaw clenched, his gaze flicking to the guards and back to her.

We're not going out like this, he murmured.

Grayson smirked, his hand inching toward the detonator on his vest. Always wanted to go out with a bang.

Mara's blood ran cold. Grayson, don't—

The explosion shook the compound, the force of it throwing them to the ground as chaos erupted around them. Mara's ears rang, her vision blurred, her body aching from the impact.

When she opened her eyes, the hallway was in shambles, smoke and debris filling the air. Nate's hand closed around hers, pulling her to her feet.

Move! he shouted.

She stumbled after him, her heart pounding as they disappeared into the chaos.

29

The Breaking Point

Smoke filled the air, thick and choking, as Mara ran through the ruined hallway. Her lungs burned, her legs felt like lead, but she didn't dare stop. Nate was ahead of her, his hand tight around hers as he pulled her through the chaos. Behind them, the shouts of guards and the echo of gunfire chased them like shadows.

Left! Nate barked, his voice sharp. They veered into a side corridor, the walls cracked and blackened from the explosion. Grayson's handiwork had been thorough, but it had also set the compound into high alert.

Where's Grayson? Mara gasped, her heart pounding.

He'll catch up, Nate said, his jaw tight. He always does.

But Mara wasn't so sure. The last she'd seen of Grayson, he'd been near the detonator. The memory of his smirk haunted her—a smirk that might have been his way of saying goodbye.

They reached a stairwell that spiraled down into darkness, the faint hum of machinery growing louder the deeper they descended. Nate slowed, his movements cautious as he scanned the area for threats.

Where are we going? Mara whispered.

Underground access tunnel, Nate replied. It's our only way out.

The sound of approaching footsteps made Mara's stomach drop. Nate grabbed her arm, pulling her behind a metal column as a group of guards stormed past, their rifles at the ready.

We're running out of time, Mara whispered.

I know, Nate said, his voice low. Stay close.

They slipped into the tunnel, its walls lined with pipes and flickering lights. The air was damp and smelled of oil, every step echoing like a gunshot in the confined space. Mara's nerves were fraying, her every sense on high alert as they moved deeper into the labyrinth.

The gunfire caught them off guard. A burst of bullets ricocheted off the walls, sending sparks flying. Mara dove behind a stack of crates, her heart hammering as she tried to catch her breath. Nate returned fire, his movements sharp and controlled, but the sheer number of attackers made it clear they were outmatched.

We're pinned! Mara shouted, her voice trembling.

Not for long, Nate said, his tone grim. He pulled something from his pocket— a small, cylindrical grenade—and lobbed it down the corridor. The explosion was deafening, the shockwave rattling the pipes above them.

When the dust settled, the corridor was eerily quiet. Nate helped Mara to her feet, his gaze flicking to the bodies sprawled on the ground.

Let's move, he said, his voice tight.

They emerged into a wide chamber, its ceiling high and crisscrossed with metal beams. In the center of the room was a control panel, its monitors flickering with data. Mara's breath hitched as she recognized the layout—it was the compound's central hub.

This is it, Nate said. Their command center.

What are we supposed to do here? Mara asked, her voice trembling.

We take it offline, Nate replied, pulling a USB drive from his pocket. If we disable their systems, we cripple their operation.

Mara nodded, stepping toward the panel. Her hands shook as she plugged in the drive, the screen filling with lines of code. The sound of her own heartbeat thundered in her ears as the progress bar inched forward.

Nate stood guard, his gun trained on the entrance. How much longer?

Two minutes, Mara said, her voice tight.

We don't have two minutes, Nate muttered, his gaze fixed on the hallway. The sound of footsteps echoed closer, the unmistakable sound of reinforcements arriving.

Mara's hands trembled as she watched the progress bar crawl forward. It's almost there!

The first guard burst through the doorway, his rifle raised. Nate fired, taking him down, but more followed, their shouts filling the air. Mara ducked as bullets tore through the room, her heart racing.

Nate! she screamed.

Keep going! he shouted back, his voice firm. Don't stop!

The progress bar hit 100%, and the screen went black. Mara yanked the USB drive free, her pulse pounding as she turned to Nate. It's done!

Then let's go! he said, grabbing her arm.

They sprinted toward the far end of the chamber, their path blocked by another wave of guards. Nate fired relentlessly, his movements precise, but the odds were against them.

A sudden explosion rocked the chamber, throwing them to the ground. Mara's ears rang as she scrambled to her knees, her vision blurred by smoke and debris.

Go! a voice shouted.

Mara turned to see Grayson, his face streaked with soot, standing in the doorway with a detonator in his hand. His grin was wild, his eyes alight with adrenaline.

Grayson! she cried.

Get out of here! he shouted. I'll hold them off!

No! Mara screamed, scrambling toward him, but Nate grabbed her, pulling her back.

He's buying us time! Nate said, his voice cracking. We have to go!

Mara fought against him, tears streaming down her face. We can't leave him!

Grayson winked at her, his grin widening. See you on the other side, sweetheart.

The explosion that followed was deafening, the force of it throwing Mara and Nate through the exit. The last thing she saw before the world went black was the fire consuming the chamber, Grayson's figure lost in the flames.

When Mara opened her eyes, the sky was dark, the stars faint and distant above the forest. She blinked, her head pounding as she tried to sit up. Nate was beside her, his face streaked with dirt and blood, his expression hollow.

Grayson, she whispered, her throat raw.

Nate shook his head, his gaze distant. He didn't make it.

Mara's chest tightened, a sob breaking free as the weight of everything crashed down on her. Grayson was gone. The mission was over, but the cost was unbearable.

Nate pulled her into his arms, his voice breaking as he whispered, We'll finish this. For him.

Mara clung to him, her tears soaking his shirt. The fight wasn't over. The network wasn't completely destroyed.

But they would see it through—no matter the cost.

30

The Final Reckoning

The days that followed Grayson's sacrifice passed in a blur. Mara and Nate holed up in a remote cabin nestled deep in the mountains, the world outside a stark contrast to the storm raging within them. The loss of Grayson was a wound neither spoke of aloud, but it was ever-present, an ache that neither time nor distance could dull.

Nate sat at the cabin's small table, his laptop open in front of him. The screen glowed with rows of code and maps, the remnants of the data they'd pulled from Pierce's files. His shoulders were tense, his face illuminated by the cold blue light.

Mara watched him from the other side of the room, her chest tightening as she took in the lines of exhaustion etched into his face. Grayson's absence was a gaping hole in their already fragile team, and the burden of their mission seemed heavier than ever.

You need to rest, she said softly, breaking the silence.

Nate didn't look up. We're not done yet.

Mara crossed the room, placing a hand on his shoulder. You're going to burn out before we even get there.

He finally met her gaze, his blue eyes shadowed but steady. This is it, Mara. The last piece. If we take down the compound they've regrouped at, the network collapses. No leaders, no resources, no infrastructure.

And no one left to fight, Mara said, her voice trembling. Not even us.

We'll survive, Nate said, his voice quiet but firm. We have to.

The final location was buried deep in the Rockies, a secluded stronghold accessible only by a single winding road. Nate had traced it through encrypted communications and supply chain anomalies—a fortress hidden from the world, where the remnants of the network's leadership had gathered like rats in a sinking ship.

We go in at night, Nate said as they loaded their gear into the truck. Hit their main generator first. Without power, their defenses will be crippled.

And then what? Mara asked, her nerves fraying at the edges.

We take them out, Nate said. All of them.

Mara nodded, swallowing hard. The enormity of what they were about to do weighed on her like a physical force, but she couldn't back down. Not now. Not after everything they'd lost.

The drive to the compound was long and silent, the winding road shrouded in darkness. Mara gripped her gun tightly, her palms damp with sweat as the truck climbed higher into the mountains. The air was cold and thin, each breath sharp against her lungs.

When the compound finally came into view, her stomach turned. It was massive, a sprawling network of buildings surrounded by high walls and watchtowers. Floodlights swept the perimeter, their beams cutting through the darkness like knives.

Nate pulled the truck into a shadowed alcove, killing the engine. He turned to Mara, his face set with grim determination.

This is it, he said. Are you ready?

No, she admitted, her voice trembling. But I'll do it anyway.

He reached out, his hand brushing hers. We finish this together.

They approached the compound under the cover of darkness, their movements silent and precise. The first obstacle was the generator—an enormous machine housed in a reinforced building at the edge of the compound. Nate set the charges while Mara kept watch, her heart pounding with every distant shout and crunch of boots on gravel.

Ready, Nate whispered, his voice barely audible.

Mara nodded, following him as they slipped back into the shadows. The explosion that followed was deafening, the blast shaking the ground beneath them. The compound was plunged into darkness, the floodlights extinguished in an instant.

Chaos erupted as guards scrambled to respond. Nate and Mara moved quickly, navigating the confusion with practiced efficiency. Their goal was the central building, where the remaining leaders of the network were believed to be holed up.

Inside, the compound was a maze of darkened hallways and echoing footsteps. Mara's nerves were raw, her every sense heightened as they crept toward the main office. The tension between them was unspoken but palpable, their movements perfectly synchronized as they worked their way through the building.

When they reached the office, Nate motioned for Mara to stay back. He pushed the door open, his gun raised, his body tense.

Inside, three figures sat at a long table, their faces illuminated by the glow of emergency lights. One of them stood as Nate entered, his expression hard.

Nathaniel Westwood, the man said, his voice calm. I wondered when you'd show up.

Then you know why I'm here, Nate said, his voice cold.

To finish what you started, the man replied. But you should know, it doesn't end with us. The network will survive. It always does.

Not this time, Nate said. This is where it ends.

The fight that followed was brutal, a whirlwind of gunfire and chaos. Mara fired at one of the leaders, her hands steady despite the terror clawing at her chest. Nate moved like a predator, his every shot precise and deadly.

When the dust settled, the room was silent. The bodies of the network's remaining leaders lay crumpled on the floor, the table overturned, blood pooling on the tiles. Mara leaned against the wall, her breath coming in ragged gasps as she tried to process what they'd just done.

It's over, Nate said, his voice soft.

Mara met his gaze, her chest tightening. Is it?

Nate hesitated, his shoulders sagging as the weight of everything they'd endured finally caught up to him. It has to be.

The dawn broke as they descended the mountain, the first rays of sunlight piercing through the trees. Mara sat in the truck, staring out the window as the landscape blurred past. The fight was over. The network was destroyed.

But the scars it had left behind would never fully heal.

We did it, Nate said, his voice quiet but firm.

Mara turned to him, her expression unreadable. What happens now?

He glanced at her, a faint smile tugging at his lips. We start over. Figure out what life looks like without all of this.

And if they come back? she asked, her voice trembling.

They won't, he said. Not after this.

Mara nodded, her heart aching with both relief and uncertainty. They'd won, but at a cost neither of them could fully comprehend.

As the truck rumbled down the mountain, Mara leaned her head against the window, her eyes closing against the rising sun. The fight was over, but the journey was far from finished.

They'd survived. And that was enough.

For now.

31

Epilogue: What Remains

The cabin was quiet, the kind of quiet that felt fragile, like the world itself was holding its breath. A fire crackled in the hearth, its warmth a welcome reprieve from the chill of the early winter morning. Mara sat at the window, her gaze fixed on the snow-dusted trees beyond. In her lap was a photo—creased and smudged from being handled too many times. It was of Grayson, his trademark smirk frozen in a moment of mischief, a memory of a man who'd burned as brightly as he'd lived.

Nate's footsteps were soft as he entered the room, his presence steady and grounding. He carried two mugs of coffee, setting one down beside her before taking a seat across the table. For a moment, they sat in companionable silence, the unspoken weight of everything they'd endured hanging between them.

How are you feeling? he asked, his voice gentle.

Mara looked at him, her lips curving into a faint, bittersweet smile. I don't know. Lighter, maybe. But also... heavier.

Nate nodded, his gaze dropping to the mug in his hands. It's strange, isn't it? To have the fight behind us.

Is it behind us? she asked, her tone uncertain. Or are we just waiting for the next storm?

There won't be a next storm, Nate said firmly. The network's gone. We made sure of that.

And what about the people who propped it up? The ones in power who let it thrive? Her voice wavered, the bitterness she'd tried to suppress slipping through. We didn't touch them.

Nate's jaw tightened, the firelight casting shadows across his face. We did what we could, Mara. And maybe... maybe it's not our fight anymore.

She studied him, her chest tightening. Do you really believe that?

He hesitated, his blue eyes meeting hers. I don't know. But I do know that we need to live. For Grayson, for ourselves. We need to figure out who we are without all of this.

Mara nodded, her fingers brushing the edge of the photo in her lap. It's hard to imagine what that looks like.

Maybe it looks like this, Nate said, gesturing to the cabin, the fire, the snow falling softly outside. Quiet. Simple.

She smiled faintly, her heart aching at the thought. Do you think we deserve that?

I think we've earned it, he said, his voice steady. And I think Grayson would agree.

Later, as the sun climbed higher, Mara found herself walking along the edge of the forest, her breath visible in the cold air. The crisp snow crunched beneath her boots, the silence broken only by the occasional chirp of a bird. For the first time in what felt like years, the weight in her chest eased. The danger, the running, the constant fight for survival—it was over.

When she reached the edge of a frozen stream, she stopped, her reflection wavering in the ice. She thought of all they'd lost, all they'd sacrificed. Grayson's laughter, Pierce's taunts, Shaw's smirk—ghosts that would haunt her for the rest of her life. But she also thought of Nate's unwavering determination, the way he'd pulled her back from the edge time and time again.

You okay? Nate's voice came from behind her.

She turned to see him standing a few feet away, his hands tucked into his jacket pockets. His breath fogged in the air, his expression cautious but hopeful.

I'm getting there, she said honestly.

He stepped closer, his presence a balm against the lingering ache in her chest. We'll figure it out. Together.

Mara smiled, her heart aching and healing all at once. Together.

Weeks turned into months, and slowly, life began to take shape. The cabin became their refuge, a place to rebuild and redefine who they were. Mara started painting again, her canvases filled with images of the mountains, the forest, the memories she refused to let fade. Nate found solace in the mundane—chopping wood, fixing the roof, writing in a journal he never let her read.

They didn't talk much about the past, but when they did, it was with a kind of reverence, as though the pain and the loss were sacred in their own way.

Grayson's name came up often, his memory a thread that tied them together.

He'd hate this, Mara said one evening, gesturing to the quiet cabin as they sat by the fire. The stillness, the routine.

Nate chuckled, his smile tinged with sadness. Yeah. He'd call us boring and drag us off on some reckless adventure.

Probably, she agreed, her laughter soft.

But even as they joked, they both knew the truth: Grayson had given them this chance. And they wouldn't waste it.

One morning, months later, a letter arrived—a rare occurrence in their isolated world. It was from a journalist, someone who'd been following the breadcrumbs they'd left behind. The network's collapse had sent shockwaves through the underworld and beyond, exposing corruption at the highest levels. Investigations had begun. Arrests were being made.

Mara read the letter aloud, her voice trembling with a mix of disbelief and vindication. When she finished, she looked at Nate, her eyes shining.

We did it, she said softly.

He nodded, his expression calm but his eyes betraying his own quiet relief. Yeah. We did.

For the first time in a long time, Mara felt the weight lift completely. The fight was truly over. And now, they could finally begin to live.

As the snow began to fall again, blanketing the cabin and the forest in a peaceful hush, Mara and Nate stood together at the edge of the stream. The world felt open, vast, and full of possibility. For the first time, the future didn't feel like something to fear.

It felt like a gift.

And they were ready to take it.

www.ingramcontent.com/pod-product-compliance
Lightning Source LLC
Chambersburg PA
CBHW070615120726
47909CB00004B/1222